THE FIXER'S MESS

THE FIXER'S MESS

Orr Agam

Library of Congress Control Number: 2020924425
ISBN: Hardcover   978-1-6641-4683-9
                Softcover   978-1-6641-4682-2
                eBook   978-1-6641-4681-5

Rev. date: 12/17/2020

To order additional copies of this book, contact:
Xlibris
844-714-8691
www.Xlibris.com
Orders@Xlibris.com
801341

To my mother,
Nitza,
and
father,
Ofer,
for their unconditional love and constant support.

CONTENTS

PART I
The Fixer

PART II
The Mess

PART III
The Fix

PART I

The Fixer

CHAPTER 1

Personal Lawyer

San Francisco, California

1.

I did not get on a fucking red-eye from New York to be treated like an asshole. If his only intention was to humiliate me and throw me out of his office like a dog, I ought to have a good night's sleep. What kind of person demands that his lawyer urgently fly cross-country just to be yelled at in person rather than over the phone? A narcissistic psychopath compelled to prove his control and domination over my body and soul. I was used to being a frequent target of his temper tantrums, but to be called an incompetent prick without having slept a wink was another thing altogether. I would have paid anything to have punched him in his bulgy stomach and see his disheveled "blond" hair and crinkly red face writhing in pain. Even as this fantasy played in my mind, I knew I was kidding myself. I loved the bastard, and he knew it. He could shoot someone in the middle of Fifth Avenue, and I would still support him.

San Francisco sits near cold ocean waters, which brings in wind and fog during the summer, making it the coldest city in America during this time. So, despite it being the middle of July, I was freezing my tuchus off without anywhere to go. My only client, Duncan Thomas, deemed this necessary punishment for the lousy job I had done with my "assignment." Being one of the biggest hotel magnates in the world, Duncan had blacklisted me from all his hotel properties. He'd even made sure his hotel mogul friends followed suit. Most people would not be so petty to go to these extremes just to prove a point, but no one on this planet was like Duncan.

The little whore wouldn't accept the offer. Was I supposed to *make* her take the money? Did Duncan expect me to put a gun to her head and make her sign the paper in front of me like some mobster? Was it possible that he expected those "activities" from me? Hopefully, that question did not need an answer anytime soon. I had said vicious things to a lot of people on Duncan's behalf, including threats of violence, but I had never actually followed through with them. If he did not think I was up to the job, I suppose he could find someone else to take care of this particular mess. That would hurt me professionally and emotionally. But if I were completely honest, it would also be a huge relief. I enjoyed playing a tough guy, but I had been brought up to be a good Jewish boy from Brooklyn.

I ordered a ride to some cheap shithole located at Ocean Beach. In New York, I got to places sitting in the back of a yellow taxi. I appreciated the smell of leather seats and the barrier between the driver and the rider. There was something nice about knowing exactly what you were going to get. These days, I order an *Uber* from my phone, and any type of crappy car could show up. This ride-sharing garbage just wasn't for me, but there weren't too many cabs left, especially in this city.

It was freezing next to the ocean when I arrived at my small motel. It was not the Ritz, but at least I could fall asleep to the sound of the huge Pacific waves. I had been in such a rush when I'd *schlepped* here from New York that I hadn't had time to pack any luggage. The only clothes I had on me were the custom Italian suit and shoes I was wearing. I asked the kid working the desk for slippers and a bathrobe. He shrugged and gave me a bunch of hand towels and a flattened box of cardboard instead.

Too tired and upset to care how small my room was, I slipped into my makeshift robe and collapsed on the shabby twin single bed. I attempted to sleep, but after five minutes, I decided it was a futile effort. I was still pissed about Duncan's outburst but also worried he had not reached out since then. Calling him was out of the question. It would make me look weak, and Duncan hated weakness more than anything—except disloyalty.

Should I try with the stupid bitch again? If it were to go sideways, I would be in trouble with not only Duncan but also the law. And as I was a lawyer, the latter came with severe consequences, particularly in this city, since I'd received my juris doctorate from Golden Gate Bridge Law School of San Francisco. It was actually through my school connections that I met Duncan. In the intervening years between then and now, a lot of bullshit happened, most of which was better forgotten—for Duncan and me.

Along with a pair of sandals and large black sweatpants, I bought a T-shirt with an animated drawing of the city, a cartoon heart in the middle and a caption—"I left my heart in San Francisco"—from a nearby thrift store on Taraval. I looked like a *putz*, but in San Francisco, this attire was acceptable. If I wore these clothes in Manhattan, New Yorkers would either hand me their loose change or yell at me to "get a job already." I was so anxious anticipating Duncan's call that I walked the boardwalk to relax. I was struck how lost I was without Duncan, even for the short time it had been since he'd thrown me out on my ass. Luckily, I didn't have the luxury to contemplate what that signified about me right now.

I traveled farther uphill past the end of the boardwalk to Lands End. Instead of appreciating the beautiful view of the Sutro Baths perfectly placed in front of the Pacific Ocean, I checked my phone and saw Duncan had not called or texted. Suddenly, I felt a tingle slowly rise from my feet to my chest, along with a feverish forehead and a developing cold sweat.

My phone chimed, alerting me I'd received a text from Duncan. He demanded I "come the hell back" to his hotel immediately. The tingling vanished as fast as it had appeared. I ran down back toward my motel to put on my suit and receive my marching orders from Duncan.

2.

"I said cash! Why didn't we pay with cash?"

Duncan's face notoriously turned ruby red when he yelled in frustration, and he was frustrated most of the time. Duncan functioned in three moods—happy, angry, and horny. In every mood, he was a humongous asshole. If he was angry at the same entity you were, there was no one you'd rather have on your side in a fight. On the flip side, if you were on the other (in other words, the short) end of the stick, it was preferable to be anyone else in the known universe.

"She took the money. I wouldn't worry about it—"

"What the fuck did you say? Are you telling me not to worry?" Duncan yelled, verbally cutting off my head midsentence.

"Look," I said, squirming in my seat, "I'm going to fix this. That is what I do. I fix things for you. That is why I am telling you—I mean, suggesting for you—not to worry."

"Shove your suggestion up your ass, Max! You don't fix things. You just make a mess, and this time, you fucked me!" Duncan shook his head in disgust.

"I'm sorry, boss. I thought cash would seem inappropriate. The only reason people pay with cash is so it can't be traced, which is a red flag of something criminal. That's why I thought we set up the payment through official means."

"How do you trace cash? The whole point of paying in cash is so you can't trace it!"

I didn't feel like explaining that a deposit and subsequent withdrawal of $300,000 could not be legally hidden. You would think someone who manages hotels and cash flow would be aware of this. Sometimes, I was not sure if he *was* obtuse or just acting like it for convenience's sake.

"What do you want me to do, boss?" I asked.

"I want you to fix it! Are you my fixer or not?"

"Yes, boss. I'm your guy. I know just what to do," I assured him, without actually having a clue.

"Good, good, good. Glad to hear it." He smiled. "You are my number one guy, Max. You know that, right? There is no one in the world I trust more than you, okay? That is why I need you in this delicate manner. I need you to fix it."

Only Duncan could cause me to go from nearly shitting my pants to feeling like royalty in the next sentence. I was aware I was being manipulated to do what Duncan desired, but I could not help but feel self-assured and confident after receiving his praise. In Duncan's warped world, everyone associated with him was his slave, with complete obedience and total loyalty required at all times.

3.

More and more, I wondered why I was so willing and able to put up with Duncan's bullshit. Could it simply be my admiration for Duncan's ambition and success? Initially, I'd thought I could learn from him and become a "Duncan"-type businessman in the (hopefully near) future. I learned to treat people I deemed as "weak" with disrespect and targeted rage, without regard or consequence. I'd always had this urge to be this tough-guy prick. I'd never acted on it before I'd met Duncan, but that didn't mean it wasn't there.

Speaking of which, it was time to bust some heads together, figuratively speaking (for now). The broad might have spoken against Duncan with some swagger and confidence to the reporter, but she was scared. The last time we spoke, it was clear she was petrified of Duncan. Though I was officially unaware of the specifics of their relationship, if history was any indicator, it involved a lewd act. It was too soon to confront her again. She might do something rash she (and consequently I) would regret. Better to start with the reporter. She would also be reluctant to talk to me, but being the eager beaver journalist that she was, she would answer my call.

Sarah Verand worked for the *New Jersey News*. It was a newspaper out of Jersey, so I usually would give two shits about it. However, Duncan was concerned the prestigious New York papers would pick up the story due to their proximity. In the past, Sarah had cozied up to Duncan to ride his fame to further her career, something Duncan didn't mind in the least, as long as he was "taken care of" in return. He loved getting press coverage, even negative coverage, but that did not mean he *liked* all the coverage. The story Sarah was about to break would be the type of coverage Duncan detested. I was not sure why Sarah would turn on Duncan, but I was not surprised either. In Duncan's world, people tended to waver from his good side to his bad side. Sarah might not know it yet, but she had just gotten on the wrong end of the Duncan stick.

As I predicted, she answered my call after the third ring. "Hello?"

"Hey, Sarah. It's Max Cedar. What's this I hear about a story you're writing about Duncan?"

"Who told you I'm doing a story about Duncan?" she responded defensively. She was caught off guard that I knew what she was up to, and she was on her proverbial heels, creating an opening for me to move more aggressively.

"Listen, trash this piece. Duncan will give you an exclusive on this new hotel opening in Dubai. It's going to be amazing. We'll fly you out there first class. You'll be treated like the established reporter that you are—great room, great food, and great people. Does that sound like something you might be interested in?"

"Oh, well, that sounds great, Max," Sarah responded in a surprised tone.

"That's good to hear. I cannot tell you how happy I am that we came to an understanding on this. Duncan is going to be pleased that we were able to smooth this one over."

"Well—" she started.

"You just said we were all set a second ago," I snapped.

"Listen, Max, this is a big exclusive. And if I don't break it, someone else will. But seeing how nice your offer is, I can allow Duncan an opportunity to respond," she replied.

"Don't worry about what other people are going to do. Just worry about what you are going to do—or, in this case, what you're not going to do. You will not publish that story, and then you're going to have the most wonderful time in Dubai. Does that fully clarify what you are going to do now?"

"Max, with all due respect to you and Duncan, I choose what stories I write."

"No."

"No what?"

"No, you don't choose the stories you write, at least not about Duncan. You ask me if you can write a story about Duncan, and I tell you if you can or not. That is what you should have done when this lying whore came to you in the first place."

"This conversation is over. Tell Duncan thanks for the offer, but I'm going to proceed with the story how I wish. You don't tell me what I can or can't write about," she retorted.

"I'm going to tell Duncan that Sarah is trashing the story. You got that? If I read that fucking story in your shit rag of a paper, I'm going to mess your career up so badly that you won't even be able to recognize it again, so get that through your thick fucking skull. This story will never be printed, shared, videotaped—not a fucking thing. Tread lightly on this one, Sarah."

"What is that supposed to mean?"

"It means think about your career. Think about the hours in court and the money for lawyers you're going to need to spend. Think about how your life is going to be completely fucked from this, okay? This story is done. It will not be published! If it is, what will happen to you will be completely disgusting!"

"Okay, Max. I will not be intimidated. If you have nothing to add for the article—"

"There is nothing to add because there is no fucking article, understand?" I screamed into the phone. "It will be my pleasure to ruin you and your paper, but I won't need to because there is no article. That's it. No more discussion on this. Be smart, Sarah!"

I hung up before she was able to respond. As I wiped my spit from my chin, I felt an adrenaline high surged throughout my body. I wanted to take on King Kong, Godzilla, and any other monster dumb enough to mess with me. Any guilt over verbally abusing a reporter, especially a woman, drowned in the waves of power that washed over me. Besides, why should I feel guilty? I'd offered Sarah a carrot with a sweet offer to drop the story. Was it my fault she refused it? Furthermore, Sarah was a professional. I was sure we could reconcile in the future. After all, I was just following orders.

I bought a fifth of Jack whiskey before returning to my motel room. It was celebratory drinking—the alternative reason dismissed out of hand. Duncan had never felt any remorse for treating people like shit. Inevitably, unnecessary feelings like guilt and shame would subside for me also.

Half a bottle later, I received a text message from Duncan: "You are big-time, Max! I knew you could handle it. I still need you to follow up with London. Make sure she won't blab to another reporter. Scummy media always trying to destroy me! The penthouse is yours! Top-level, Max!"

Duncan's penthouse offer at one of the best hotels in San Francisco was tempting. However, as dingy as this motel was, it was nice to have space from Duncan. Anyway, I shouldn't be dependent on him for a room to sleep in after being thrown out on my ass the other night.

I took a stroll on the boardwalk after I finished the bottle and gazed at the sun setting. The whiskey kept me warm in the blistering cold. I took off my shoes and walked on the cold sand. Before I knew it, my lower body was covered in the freezing water, with light waves splashing my face. The orange sun was disappearing from the purple sky. It looked apocalyptic. I wondered if the world could end in such a peaceful way—quiet ocean waves, purple skies, and a fading sun while the earth imploded.

4.

I was positive I was having a stroke early the next morning. My chest burned like Chernobyl, complemented by severe tightness from my left jaw. This was not the first time I'd experienced these symptoms. I had been to the hospital several times before for signs of a stroke. My doctor had always told me it was very likely a panic attack and/or severe acid indigestion from heavy drinking. Nonetheless, I was convinced this time it was a stroke. I jotted down my symptoms so I could give it to the attending doctor if I ended up in the hospital:

1. I am having difficulty breathing deep breaths.
2. I have a tingly feeling on my left arm between my elbow and hand.
3. I have occasional numbness on the left side of my jaw.
4. I had a thought and tried to express it but was unable to speak.
5. I feel a bit loopy, though not so loopy I cannot think clearly.
6. I have a stingy feeling in my right temple.
7. My legs feel weightless and then heavy a minute later.

In case it was a panic attack, I figured a walk on the boardwalk would help. With the ocean breeze behind me, I breathed in the fresh air on this rare sunny San Francisco summer day. My chest pain became fainter with every step I took. Even the tightness in my jaw began to loosen up. Maybe it was just a rough hangover. Lying in the ocean for such a long time may have contributed to how I'd felt earlier in the morning. These explanations may be more probable causes for my chest pain and light-headedness than a stroke, though I still was not entirely convinced.

I felt rejuvenated when I reached the end of the boardwalk, and then my phone rang. It was Duncan. My chest began to burn again.

"Where the hell are you?" Duncan screamed into the phone.

"Where am I? I'm at Ocean Beach."

"Are you kidding me? It's a fucking disaster here, and you're having a day at the beach?"

"Well, that is where my motel is."

"Get the sand out of your ass, Max! Get the hell down here right now!"

"What is the emergency?"

"That bitch reporter wrote the story. It's all over the news. You said you fixed it!"

"I swear I did. I can't believe she went through with it."

"Did you talk to London yet?"

"No, I was going to do that today."

"Holy shit! What the hell is wrong with you? Go talk to her right now!"

"I thought you said the story is already printed."

"She hasn't confirmed anything yet! There is still time for you to fix this shitstorm of yours. Go talk to her immediately! And make sure that lying reporter doesn't write another word about this!"

"Okay, boss. I'm on it. I'm going to see London right now."

"Don't fuck it up this time!" Duncan yelled before he abruptly hung up the call.

I ran back to the motel. When I entered my motel room, I looked at my phone for the last address I had for London. While scrolling through my phone, my chest pain came roaring back.

5.

I didn't have time to go to the hospital before paying a visit to London. Instead, I made a stop at one of the several local recreational marijuana dispensaries. I had recently read that high concentrates of CBD could prevent the onset of strokes. The cute weed barista girl convinced me to buy five chocolate chip cookies, each one containing 100 mg of CBD. She suggested a cannabis oil vaporizer with a CBD oil pod for my chest pains as well. She demonstrated how all I had to do was inhale to turn it on. I bought three of those. I scarfed down a cookie and inhaled my vaporizer at a rapid pace as I headed toward London's place, which was located a couple of miles away at the Park Merced Apartment Complexes.

Even though it was midday, the residents of the complex were shuffling in and out. Mainly senior citizens or college students resided here, and both seemed to have similar daily schedules. I had no idea what to say to London. After my experience with Sarah Verand, my preference was not to be hostile. But if she decided to confirm Sarah's report, I would not have another option.

I knew where London lived from working out the payment to keep her mouth shut in the first place. If you had told me back then that she was going to spill the beans and be fined a million dollars for breaking the nondisclosure agreement she'd signed, I would have laughed. Now I was about to confront London for doing just that, and it sure as hell was no laughing matter. There was a good chance she was home because she worked exclusively at night.

I knew London would try to avoid me at all costs, so I covered the peephole with my thumb before knocking on the door in the style of a deliveryman. No one wants to miss a package and go to the post office to pick it up. I heard London scurry toward the door, followed by the unlocking click sound before the door swung open.

The look on her face reminded me of the cute girl in that horror movie when she realizes the killer was inside the house. Her pale skin turned another shade of white; her brown eyes narrowed on me like a locked and loaded pistol. She was wearing a white bathrobe with her hair wrapped in a towel. For such a little lady, she had quite the physique, particularly her chest, which was more than enough for Duncan to pursue her in an aggressive and sustained manner. She tried to slam the door in my face, but I caught it right before it closed, nearly breaking my ring finger in the process.

"Get the hell out of here, Max, or I'll call the police!" London yelled. "I got nothing to say to you or your fat fucking boss!"

"Nice to see you as well, London," I said with a forced smile. "I just need to ask you one question."

"I don't need to answer any questions or listen to any more of your bullshit!" she hollered and attempted to close the door again. I held the door open forcefully but was careful not to enter the apartment without an invitation.

"I just want to make sure you don't do anything stupid. I know you might be mad at Duncan—"

"Mad? I don't give a shit about him, one way or the other. He can drop dead for all I care," she said.

"Great. We just want to make sure you don't say something that could cost you a lot of money. That's all."

"What the hell are you going on about?"

"You know what. Forget it. You don't want me here. I'm just trying to make sure you don't lose a million dollars," I told her and slowly turned to leave.

"Wait," she said in a much more engaging tone. "What million dollars?"

"The million dollars you are going to have to pay if you break the NDA you signed about you and Duncan by talking to that idiot reporter."

London's facial expression slowly changed from shock to frustration. "She knew about me and Duncan on her own! She called me to confirm it. That's all."

"And what did you say?"

"I didn't say anything."

"Bullshit."

"What bullshit?"

"Who else knows about you two? You must have told her."

"Why would I do that?"

"Who the hell knows? Maybe you're trying to get more money out of Duncan."

"I swear I didn't tell her! I don't know how she knew, but she fucking knows!"

"Who told her?"

"She wouldn't tell me."

"Who did you tell?"

"What do you mean?"

"Who knows about you and Duncan? Come on already!"

"Just your dumb ass, okay? I didn't tell anyone else."

"Someone told somebody something."

"Not me."

London's story made no sense. I had to get the record straight, and it was not going to come from her. Flustered, I threw my hands up and walked away.

"What about the money?" she asked.

"I'll talk to Duncan," I replied.

Duncan would not want to pay more money, but if it was necessary to put this *meshugas* behind him, he would. Besides, London asking for more money was the least of our problems. First and foremost, I had to find out who the hell was leaking the goods on Duncan's sex life.

6.

Based on our last conversation, I couldn't say I was surprised Sarah ignored over a dozen of my calls. Surely, this was a consequence of my aggressive behavior exhibited toward her the day before, but I had no time to reflect on my business tactics. I needed to find out who'd told her about

Duncan and London. It sure as hell wasn't me. And if it wasn't London, then it must have been Duncan inadvertently. I dreaded telling Duncan this theory, so I texted Sarah in desperation. "Hey, sorry about the last time we spoke. If you can call me, I would like to remedy this situation between us. Please let me know when you are available to chat."

A thick fog had replaced the sun the mere minutes I spoke with London. I inserted a new CBD cartridge and inhaled it like a vacuum cleaner, to the point I nearly finished it by the time the car arrived to take me to Duncan's hotel. I requested that my driver stop by the weed dispensary on the way to Duncan's, and the driver told me I needed to log it in through my phone.

I told him, "That is so fucking stupid," and handed him twenty dollars to make the stop at the Green Crow Dispensary anyway.

I bought five more vaporizer cartridges and five more weed cookies. I gave the driver an additional twenty for allowing me to smoke the vaporizer in the car. I was high as a kite when I arrived at Duncan's hotel, but my eyes weren't too red, and I still looked sharp as a tack. I knew doing business stoned was not a good idea, but there were certain instances when dealing with Duncan where it was essential.

The front desk security waved me through shaking his head. This was his warning to me that Duncan was in one of his extreme temper tantrums. I considered turning around and heading for the hills, but I bravely entered the elevator to face my doom. I heard Duncan screaming through the closed door when the elevator doors opened at Duncan's floor.

"I don't give a shit!" Duncan shouted into his big landline phone. He had a cell phone, but he always liked the look of sitting behind a desk with a huge phone; it was "stylish" in the 1980s.

"So tell him to fuck off! I don't care if he says he's going to sue me. I'll sue his ass for a lot more. And another thing, I'm going to sue his ass for a lot more money!" Duncan shouted.

"Okay, whatever you say, Duncan," a middle-aged male voice replied through the speakerphone. I recognized the voice as belonging to Joel, his real estate lawyer.

"Damn right! Send him a damn message to him so he knows!"

"Okay, but you should know he isn't just going to take it. He's going to fight back, and he isn't afraid of a court battle."

Duncan hung up the phone before Joel could finish his sentence. Duncan paced back and forth the length of his desk, clearly still frustrated from the phone call. I did my best not to make eye contact before he settled down.

"Anything I should know about?" I asked, my eyes still glued to the floor.

"What? You? You'll just screw it all up," he said while still pacing. Though the remark appeared to be off the cuff, it stung like a dagger to the heart. I was certain he intended to have that effect.

"Well, I spoke to London."

Duncan immediately stopped pacing. "You did? When? Where?"

"An hour ago … at her apartment."

"Why did you go to her apartment?"

"You told me to go talk to her."

"Anyone see you there?"

"Only people there are senior citizens who can barely remember what they had for lunch," I told him.

This elicited a smirk from Duncan. He sat back down at his large desk. "So what did she have to say?" he asked.

"She says she didn't say anything to anyone," I answered.

"Then who told Sarah?"

"She says she doesn't know."

"You believe her?"

"I never believe anything she says, but she didn't seem like she was looking for trouble. She told me Sarah only called to confirm the story. So someone had already told Sarah the details of your relationship with London."

"And did she?"

"Did she what?"

"Confirm the story?"

"No."

"What else did she say?"

"She asked for more money."

"What a nasty woman."

"If she had broken the contract, I don't think she would ask for more money to *remain* quiet. So it is not all bad news."

"How much?"

"I think ten thousand should be more than enough."

"Okay, pay her, but in *cash* this time. Got it?"

"Yes, boss."

"We need to talk to Sarah before this story comes out."

"One hundred percent agree, boss."

Duncan gazed out to the view of the downtown skyscrapers of San Francisco. Duncan took tremendous pride that he owned the tallest building in the city—until Daniel Siminayoff had built his Skyforce Offices a couple of stories taller than Duncan's hotel last year. Regardless, Duncan still maintained his building was the tallest.

"Okay. I'll deal with it," Duncan said.

"You sure?" I asked

"Yeah, you did what you could. I'll take it from here," Duncan replied.

"Okay. I'll see myself out."

Before I exited the office, Duncan immediately picked up his huge phone and dialed some numbers. It was tough to know if he was indeed calling someone or simply a muscle reflex to pick up the phone when anyone left his office.

7.

The mist was so thick the following morning it was like walking through clouds on the boardwalk. Despite not an inch of sunshine, I wore my sunglasses to keep the sand out of my eyes from the strong crosswinds. After a mile down the Great Highway, I couldn't take it anymore and headed across the street to a local café in hopes of waiting out the fog. While I sipped my coffee, I pondered why Duncan had dismissed me from the mission at hand. Why would he risk getting directly implicated in this shit? What did he not want me to know? By the time I finished my coffee, my head pounded as thoughts spiraled in my mind—and still no fucking sunshine. I should have brought my vaporizer with me.

In the meantime, I needed to go see Larry, Duncan's accountant, aka the "cash guy." Like myself, Larry was a Jewish kid from Brooklyn. Duncan liked to hire Jews based on anti-Semitic notions. He always remarked how, "Jews are good with money," or, "Jewish lawyers are good at the shifty shit." It was tough to swallow, but compared to the racist shit he said about other minorities, the Jews got off easy.

Larry lived in the Presidio Heights, the first or second most expensive neighborhood in the city. Houses in this neighborhood got sold for millions of dollars, with some in the tens of millions. Unlike downtown, these streets were shockingly clean. City cops were constantly picking up homeless people from here and "relocating" them into the Tenderloin to maintain such high sanitary standards.

Though he told everyone he owned the house he lived in, in reality, Larry could only afford to rent the first floor from his upstairs neighbor and landlord. Nearly a foot shorter than me, his bald spot visibly reflected the light of any room he inhabited. Duncan liked him because he was brilliant; nonthreatening; and most importantly, extremely loyal to Duncan.

"You here for the money?" Larry asked, opening the door.

Though it was the late evening and Larry was home alone, he wore a buttoned white shirt and blue tie. I had never seen him without a tie on. I'd asked him once why he always had his tie on. He answered, "With Duncan, I am always working."

"As usual, Larry, you're on top of it," I told him with a cockeyed smile.

"Don't tell me what it's for," he reminded me.

"Just as long as you don't tell me how you got it," I replied.

I plopped down in the middle of his small couch, while Larry retrieved the money from the safe. The lock was modern, requiring fingerprint, facial, and voice verification to disarm it. If that weren't enough, there was a combination that could burn everything in the safe for Larry to give in case he was being tortured. His willingness to go to such lengths to keep Duncan's money and secrets secure was why Larry had lasted nearly thirty years working for Duncan.

"Bag or briefcase?" Larry asked as he took out several stacks of bills and put them on the table.

"Briefcase—it goes better with the suit," I replied.

"Can't argue with that logic," Larry said, putting the money in a black leather suitcase. "You put in the combination yourself—up one, back twice, then up again and click."

"I better get going and get this thing done already," I said. "You have a good night."

"You too. And Duncan told me for you to be careful with the money," Larry said, pointing to the briefcase.

"You take care of yourself, Larry."

"You do the same, Max. You do the same."

I sighed in relief that this meshugas would be over after this last errand. I was headed back to New York to celebrate my father's birthday first thing in the morning. I never thought I would be so happy to get back to the sweat and heat of a New York summer, but it was just too damn cold in San Francisco.

8.

London did not answer. Nor did she respond to my numerous calls outside her apartment door. What the hell was I going to do with this money? My flight to New York was hours away. I was anxiously waiting, standing outside her door for too long. I called Duncan to see what I should do next, but the call kept on ringing without an answer. I was stuck in place with nowhere to go. It would be a bitch and a half to get back to Larry and return the money, but I didn't see another recourse.

The second I exited the lobby of London's apartment complex, a police car quickly approached me with the red-and-blue lights turned on. I assured myself that they weren't there for me but, rather, there was a problem occurring in the building.

"Max Cedar?" the police car megaphone blasted.

They were not here for a problem occurring in the building.

"Are you Max Cedar?" the voice from the megaphone asked again.

"Are you talking to me?" I yelled back.

Two male police officers exited the car slowly with their hands above their holsters.

"Max Cedar, we kindly ask you to come with us to the station," the taller officer asked.

"What for?" I barked.

"Max Cedar, please come with us," the other (shorter) officer asked, both still with their hands hovered over their weapons.

"Are you asking me to come or telling me to?" I asked.

"Get in the fucking car, Mr. Cedar," the taller one demanded.

"I am a lawyer! I know my rights!" I yelled.

"You have two choices right now. You can get in the car without cuffs and unruffled, or we can beat the shit out of you, cuff you, and arrest you for resisting arrest," the shorter officer explained.

"Am I under arrest?" I asked.

"You will be and a whole lot more if you don't get in the back of this car!"

They would undoubtedly find the cash if they pounded me to the ground, so I entered the car on my own volition.

The taller officer told me, "Good choice," before he slammed the door behind me.

Whatever was happening, there was nothing good about it.

9.

The ride was mostly silent due to the fact that, whenever I asked what the hell was going on, the officers told me to shut the fuck up. I held on to the briefcase like Jack on that wooden board in the big boat movie. Unlike that dumb bastard, I would not let go, even if that meant Rose would sink to the bottom of the ocean. I tried to figure what the hell this was all about. My gut said it had something to do with Duncan, but I couldn't be sure of anything at the moment. The car pulled into the police station, and I gingerly stepped out of the car after the officers opened my door.

"Thanks for the lift, fellas. You get five stars." I smirked.

"Follow us," the short officer directed me.

The only thing I'd found out in the car was his name—Officer Smudge. He was a mean-looking son of a bitch. With a face like that, he could only be a cop or a mobster. Unfortunately for me, he'd chosen to be a cop.

I entered the precinct confidently, but I honestly felt like throwing up all over the floor. The numbness in my right arm was back, and I was so light-headed I could faint in an instant. As a lawyer, I knew that the more nervous I appeared, the guiltier the impression was. Guilty of what exactly was still unclear.

"You'll be talking to the chief in his office," Officer Smudge said, and he opened a door.

"The chief, huh? You guys are going all out for this one," I replied.

"If that is how you want to look at it, go right ahead," Officer Smudge said.

"What's your partner's name?" I asked.

"Fuck you," Officer Smudge said.

"Officer Fuck You, huh? Is that Polish?"

"Officer Crews," the taller officer chirped.

"Officer Smudge and Officer Crews," I said. I took out my phone. "I'm just going to write that down in case I forget."

"What are you, a lawyer or something?" Officer Crews asked.

"You bet your ass I am."

"Oh, wow." Officer Smudge nudged Officer Crews. "I told you he looked like an asshole."

"When you're right, you're right." Officer Crews laughed.

"We can't all be brilliant enough to graduate security guard school," I said, wiping the smiles off the both of them.

It was not the best idea to antagonize the cops, but I had to show that I was unfazed by all this nonsense. Plus, I hadn't done anything wrong, so they could go pound sand for all I cared. However, the ten grand could get me in a tricky situation, so I was relieved to see the chief enter his office and not talk to Dumb and Dumber anymore.

"That will be all, gentlemen," the chief said to the other officers.

Officers Smudge and Crews loudly grunted before sulking away, muttering unpleasantries to each other.

"I see you made some new friends," the chief said.

"It was an unexpected introduction," I replied.

"I bet it was." The chief chuckled before being fully seated. "I'm Chief Willard Williams."

"Nice to meet you, Chief Williams."

"Please call me Will."

"Okay then, Will. What is this meeting all about?"

"Well, we have a situation, and we were hoping you could assist us by answering a couple of questions: Where were you last night? Can anyone corroborate you were with them?"

"Like an alibi? Am I under arrest?"

"Are you in cuffs? Are you in an interrogation room?"

"Am I a person of interest?"

"Unfortunately, I cannot comment on an active investigation."

"Active investigation about what? Will, with all due respect, what the hell is going on here? I am a lawyer—"

"I am aware of who and what you are. It is why you're here."

"Listen, Chief Williams, or Will, or Will Williams, I don't know what is going on here. As a lawyer, I am well aware of my rights. So if you can skip the shit and get to the point, or I'll be on my way—"

"Do you know an individual by the name of Sarah Verand?" Chief Williams interrupted me.

This is about Sarah all along? Did she report me to the police for threatening her the other day?

"Sarah Verand … the reporter?" I insincerely asked.

"So you know her?"

"I know of her, sure. She does stories on Duncan Thomas."

"Your client, correct?"

"Yes, he is."

"Your only client, right?"

"As a lawyer, I cannot divulge that information."

"You said you know of her. You never spoke to her?"

"It's possible. I have discussions with many reporters who write about Duncan."

"Sorry, it was tough to tell. Is that a yes or no?"

"It's possible."

"So you never called her?"

"Not that I can remember, but like I said, it is possible."

"Do you remember what you did yesterday?"

"You want to know what I remember from yesterday?"

"Sure, if you want to tell me. But I asked only *if* you remember, not what you remember. Do you remember what you did yesterday?"

"I don't have amnesia, if that's what you're asking."

"That's exactly what I'm asking. So you do remember? Generally speaking."

"Generally speaking, yes."

"How about two days ago? Do you remember what you did?"

"Sure. As I said, I don't have amnesia."

"You did say that," Chief Williams said as he put his hands on his desk and shrugged his shoulders. "You don't have amnesia, meaning you should be able to recall the actions and events you experienced the last two days of your life. So the question I need to ask is, Why are you unable to remember calling Sarah Verand nearly twenty times in the last forty-eight hours?"

Whatever the hell was going on, I was fucked.

"How would you know who I called? Were you tracking my calls? I hope you have a warrant for that!" I adamantly responded.

This tactic came directly from Duncan—if you're in a corner, go on the offensive, and go as hard as you can.

"Why would we track your calls?" Chief Williams asked with a condescending look. "Do you remember calling Sarah Verand now or not?"

"What's it to you? It's a free country. I'll call the Pope if I feel like it," I said.

"I didn't ask you if you called the Pope. I asked if you called Sarah Verand. You said you didn't remember calling her eighteen times in two days."

"I didn't say that."

"Do you remember calling her eighteen times?"

"Yeah, I called her. Is that illegal now?"

"What did you talk about?"

"This and that."

"About a story she was going to do on Duncan?"

"A story on Duncan? Oh yeah, we invited her out to do some piece on one of Duncan's new hotels in Dubai."

"And she said she was going to write an article about this hotel?"

"We were still discussing the details, but it sounded like she was on board, sure."

"That's not what it sounded like."

"What do you know about it?"

"Her phone was recovered fully intact. There were eighteen missed calls from you in just the past two days. It also contains a recorded conversation of you extorting, bribing, and threatening her about not revealing some scoop she has on Duncan."

"What do you mean *found*?"

"She's dead."

"Who is dead?"

"Sarah Verand was found dead yesterday in her car, parked in the lot of the very newspaper she wrote for."

I was not prepared to finish this conversation, and Chief Will Williams knew it. I had to get the hell out of here before I said anything else. I had said way too much already.

"Am I under arrest?" I asked with a slight crack in my voice.

"Why would you be? Did you do something wrong, Max? Did you kill Sarah Verand?" Chief Williams asked.

"This conversation is over. You want to talk to me again, talk to my lawyer."

"I thought you were a lawyer."

"Goodbye, Chief Will Williams!"

I walked out in such a hurry I nearly left without the briefcase—a briefcase containing ten grand to be used as Duncan's hush money and now potentially connected to an active murder investigation.

CHAPTER 2

Barney's Bagels

New York, New York

1.

I tried to drink myself to sleep during the flight back to New York. I was unsuccessful and, now, was not only anxious but also very drunk. The obese man sitting next to me was snoring so loudly I couldn't even hear the shitty sitcom that I was watching. Not that it made a difference; I was too frazzled to concentrate on that bullshit. Questions spiraled like a word tornado in my head. Internally, I went into lawyer mode and cross-examined myself:

Did you have anything to do with the mysterious death of the reporter?

I had nothing to do with the death of Sarah Verand.

Do you have a reliable alibi?

I was across the country when the murder occurred. That is an airtight alibi.

Did you ever threaten Sarah?

It might come across that way on tape, but it was simply a tough business conversation.

Have you committed illegal acts or ever threatened anyone on behalf of Duncan Thomas?

I plead the Fifth.

It would be a huge problem if the police started digging into my past, regardless of my innocence concerning the death of Sarah Verand. The "tasks" I carried out on Duncan's behalf were not only unpleasant but intermittently illegal as well. Being a lawyer, I did know better, truth be told, but I did them anyway. Maybe some other time I could talk to some shrink about why I did them, but I had bigger problems to sort out at the moment.

The cab I took from JFK to Manhattan smelled of a combination of car freshener, stale musk, and old leather; I was home at last. Something about entering this island in a yellow cab was more than sentimental; it was romantic. I could barely keep my eyes open when the cab entered the West Side Highway and drove through Central Park, finally arriving at my residence on Ninety-First and West End.

My doorman, Billy, greeted me with a warm smile.

"Can I take your bags up for you, Mr. Cedar?" Billy asked me.

"No thanks, Billy. I got it."

I still had the briefcase with the ten grand that was designated to pay London with. Duncan was not going to be happy the package had not been delivered. It was unusual for him not to check that everything had happened without incident.

I approached my apartment door full of trepidation. Unenthusiastic would be a considerable understatement about how I felt seeing my wife. We had had a rough time shortly after I'd started working for Duncan. Ironically, she was the one who'd wanted me to work for him in the first place. She wanted me to earn more money so we could move from Buffalo to Manhattan, with all the luxuries, like this very apartment that came with it. She seemed to have completely forgotten this fact. For the past few years, she barely spoke to me. Honestly, it was preferable to the complaining.

Not even the dog was there to greet me when I entered the house. It was for the better. I did not want the family to see me this *disheveled* and drunk anyhow. I haphazardly undressed before falling on "my" bed. I turned on some cable news and was drifting off to sleep when the news anchor began speaking about the death of a New Jersey reporter. The newswoman was interviewing the *New Jersey News* editor Chase Toad.

"Was the reporter working on a story that could have led to this tragedy?" the news anchor asked.

"I cannot comment on an ongoing investigation," Chase Toad replied.

"So the police are investigating? Do they think this is a murder?" she followed up.

"I cannot comment, but most perfectly healthy thirty-one-year-old women do not randomly end up dead in their cars," Chase answered.

Shit was about to hit the fan—with me right in front of it. I closed my eyes with the hopes that, when I woke up, this would all be just a dream.

2.

Zevi furiously licked my face until I woke up from my deep sleep. Too tired to swat him off me, I let the pup get his licks in for as long as he wanted. I heard Abe and Leah arguing about god knows what in the living room. My wife attempted to mediate between the two of them by threatening to not serve the special cupcakes at my father's birthday dinner. For a glorious instant, my dire situation was forgotten, and I embraced this wonderful family dynamic. How did I ever put my family life in jeopardy? My wife's facial expression as she entered the bedroom was a jarring reminder.

"You're home," she said without emotion. "I don't like the dog on the bed."

"Hello, honey. The flight was great, and I am safe and sound, Baruch HaShem," I replied, sitting up in the bed.

"I just wasn't expecting you to be here." She picked the dog off the bed in a hostile manner.

"Of course. It's my father's birthday party. I told you I would be."

"I know you did. I just didn't think you were going to come."

"You don't believe me when I tell you something?"

"Don't start with me."

"I start? I come home after being away for weeks, and I don't even get a hello?"

"Hello, my wonderful husband! It is so good to see you! It just fills me up with sunshine to have you in my presence!" she sarcastically declared.

"Okay, that's enough. I am going to say hi to the kids and then take a shower, and we can get ready to go over to my father's to celebrate his eighty-fifth birthday, and then I'll be out of your hair again."

"You think you being here is the problem and leaving is the answer?

Have you gone completely stupid in San Francisco, or is this your aging process?" she rhetorically asked and left the room with Zevi chasing after her.

When I went to see my children, my eight-year-old daughter was in the middle of beating up my six-year-old son.

"Leah, let your brother out of the headlock," I casually remarked.

"Daddy's home!" Leah yelled, immediately letting Abe out of a headlock to hug me.

Abe, still dazed, started to cry.

"Abe, come give your father a hug."

Still crying, Abe slowly walked over until I picked him up with my left arm.

"Are you happy to see your dad?" I asked.

"Yes," he meekly replied, wiping the tears from his eyes.

"Are you excited to see your *Saba* today?" I asked them both.

They both nodded in unison. Saba means grandfather in Hebrew. Since their mother was not Jewish, my dad was called Saba, and her father's grandfather was called Grandpa.

"I know he will be excited to see you guys. Where did your mother go?" I asked them.

"Walking the dog," Leah replied while she made curls with my hair.

"I thought you guys just walked the dog?"

Neither of them responded. I gently plopped them on the ground.

"I need to get ready for Saba's birthday. I don't want any more fighting from you guys for the rest of the day, okay?" I pointed my finger at each of them.

"Okay, Daddy," Leah said with a smile and ran off to her room.

"Can I watch TV?" Abe, no longer crying, asked excitedly.

"Yes, but only cartoons or sports—"

Before I could finish my sentence, he was already on the couch with the TV turned on.

I ignored my phone ringing while waiting for the shower to heat up. I needed to pretend everything was okay for tonight.

3.

Whenever I told someone that my father had survived Nazi Germany, he or she inevitably would ask, "What camp was he in?" to which I replied, "Israel."

It was a comical answer but not exactly a joke. As a child in Germany, his father (my grandfather) read *Mein Kampf* and immediately told his family, "Pack your bags. We're leaving and never coming back!" Less than a week later, the whole *mishpocha* moved from their upper-class life in Germany to the swamps of Israel. His friends and neighbors thought my grandfather was certifiably insane to do such a thing. Unfortunately, all of them would be dead within the decade. My grandfather's bold decision in the face of adversity saved his family, his heritage, and his future generations.

My father, on the other hand, was more thoughtful and discerning than my grandfather. He was petrified of making the wrong choice. Maybe he thought his father's sacrifice meant that he needed to live life to the fullest, and that meant making the right choices. Having grown up empowered, and admittedly privileged, that burden was never an issue for me. Until now, that is. I wondered what my grandfather's view would have been of the decisions I had made working for Duncan.

My father lived uptown on 109th Street and Central Park West, where Central Park and the Upper West Side end. He had lived there for nearly forty years. I was paying his rent, another factor in my having chosen to work for Duncan, though, like my wife, he now disapproved of what I did for a living. It was convenient for the two of them to reap the benefits of my job while simultaneously criticizing me for it. If they only knew the nightmare I was currently dealing with.

My family dressed nicely for the occasion. At forty-five, my wife looked great. She worked out daily and maintained a fantastic body weight for being nearly a foot shorter than me. When she glammed herself up, like she did for tonight, she appeared ten years younger than her age. The kids looked adorable—Leah in an expensive white kid dress and Abe in a short-sleeve polo that somehow he'd already stained in the two minutes since he'd been wearing it. If someone took a photo of us, they would have the impression we were a stereotypical Upper West Side family, and at least for today I was determined for it to stay that way. My father was not doing so well in the health department, and I wanted this night to be one he cherished.

The apartment had been cleaned especially for tonight. The floors glistened, and the smell of cleaning supplies was noticeable, although fading, as the smell of the dinner gradually took its place. The tablecloth I had eaten on (and repeatedly stained) as a child had the silverware, plates, and soup bowls perfectly set on top of it. Susan, my father's girlfriend, greeted us. Now in her late sixties, she had moved to New York from her home state of Alabama when her husband passed away nearly fifteen years ago. Her Southern accent was thick, though she tried to tone it down for my father's sake, since he was a bit hard of hearing and was not used to the Southern drawl. At first, I was apprehensive that she was after my father's money, which would have been a cruel joke because he didn't have much anymore. However, it had been almost ten years since they'd met, and she had turned out to be a huge comfort to him and a big help for myself as well.

"Well, hello! I was not expecting y'all for another half an hour," she said, though she was fancily dressed already. She wore these huge looped earrings that seemed to be out of an F. Scott Fitzgerald short story.

"You know Max, always afraid we'll be late," my wife replied.

"Well, if it was up to Vivian, we would be," I said. Whenever she took a dig at me, I couldn't help but respond accordingly.

"We are so happy you all came tonight," Susan said in a clear attempt to squash the quibbling. "Aren't you two just the cutest little things in the whole wide world?" she said, patting the children on the head.

"Where's Saba?" Abe asked, weaseling away from Susan.

"He's in the other room getting ready. He is very excited to see you both. He told me to give you some presents in the meantime." Susan handed Abe a Rubik's cube. "See if you can get each side the same color."

Abe had no clue what it was but eagerly grabbed it nonetheless before running off to the living room.

"And for you, my dear Leah"—Susan smiled—"he has this special book for you since you are such an adventurous little girl." Susan handed Leah a shiny new copy of *Alice in Wonderland*.

Leah jumped for joy, grabbed the book, and followed Abe while furiously flipping the pages.

"That should keep them busy while I open a bottle of wine," she said with a wink and a smile.

"That is a truly great notion," Vivian replied. "Let me help you open it."

They both headed off to the kitchen.

Susan quickly turned back to me. "Oh, Max, you can go into the bedroom and help Isaac get dressed," she ordered more than suggested.

I knocked several times before I got an answer.

"Is that Susan?" my father asked through the door.

"It's Max," I said loudly.

"Max, oh, come in, my darling son," he said. "You can button my shirt for me."

"With pleasure." I smiled.

"How is my only son doing these days?" he asked after I finished with the last button.

"Same as ever. Work has been a little stressful—"

"Why you ever agreed to work for that gonif is beyond me," my father interrupted me, throwing up his hands and shaking his head. Gonif means "thief" in Yiddish, and my dad reserved his Yiddish these days only for defamatory and vulgar language.

"You know why I took the job," I replied. "I did it for my family."

"What, for that fancy apartment of yours?" he asked incredulously.

"And the one we are in right now."

"Oh, you did it for me? You want that I should sell the apartment? Because if that means you stop working for that lying maniac, I will do it this second!" he yelled and took out the flip phone he'd had since the mid-2000s.

"Who are you calling?"

"Your cousin Jeffrey, the real estate agent. I'm telling him to put the apartment on the market right now!"

"I'm not quitting my job, but do what you want."

"If you are not quitting, then why am I selling the apartment?"

"You shouldn't."

"Then I won't." My father put his phone down. "Now help me up."

I gently took his arm and slowly assisted him to a standing position.

"Listen, Max, I just want the best for you. Now that you have your own children, I know you can understand this," he continued.

I nodded my head in sincere acknowledgment that what he said was true.

"This man, he's a shmuck. He can only bring you trouble. God knows what you have done for him already. To be honest, I can't bear to think about it. Your mother would spit in his face if she ever met him," he said.

It would have been a possibility. She hated dishonest and arrogant men, and she was not shy in expressing her contempt for this type of person.

"If I am honest with you, she would not be thrilled with the man you have become recently. I feel if she was still with us, she would have been able to prevent it," my father said, looking down to the floor in shame. He then reached up and took my face with his two hands. "I failed you, son. And for that, I must make an apology."

"Dad." I suddenly choked up. At that moment, I wanted to tell him everything that was going on—the legal jeopardy, the terrible moral choices, and the emotional toil I had been drowning in.

"Everything is fine. You don't need to worry about me," I lied to his face.

"So," he said. "Now let's see my grandchildren. It's not every day I turn eighty-five."

We entered the main room, where Leah was reading her book and Abe was close to breaking his new toy. Vivian and Susan were laughing loudly in the kitchen, likely already finished with the bottle of wine they had just opened.

"*Kinderlach!*" My grandfather yelled out to my children, arms wide open.

"Saba!" they both said in unison and dropped the book and Rubik's cube to hug him.

I could not help but smile at this precious display. Suddenly, my phone vibrated in my pocket. It was Duncan. I ignored it, determined to enjoy the evening with my family. This night, Duncan could wait.

4.

Sunday in the Upper West Side and Central Park is special. Along Broadway, there are brunch specials for nearly every restaurant, and small jazz bands play for tips throughout the entire park. It was idyllic, and early the following morning, I had a stroll with Zevi. More than that, I wanted to avoid my wife until the kids were up. My dad's party had gone over fine. But when we'd gone to bed, there might as well have been an iceberg between Vivian and me; if I'd attempted to get intimate, my penis would have had the same outcome as the *Titanic*.

I traveled through Central Park, ending up on the East Side at the Metropolitan Museum of Art. I couldn't go in because of the dog, but watching the tourists from all over the world coming and going was a treat on its own. I indulged myself with Mr. Coldy ice cream because of the intense humidity. I gave the dog the bottom half of the cone, which he ate in two seconds. On my way back home, I stopped at Barney's to get a fish-filled Sunday brunch for the family—salmon omelet with whitefish spread on an everything bagel, called an Upper West. With this triumph of a meal, I expected excitement and warm greetings.

"Where the hell were you?" Vivian asked me, barely looking up from clearing the table.

"I walked the dog and then got us some Barney's for brunch," I replied.

"For nearly three hours? Where did you walk to, New Jersey?" Vivian scowled on her way to the kitchen.

Dismayed, I plopped the food on the table. "Where are the kids?"

"They ate already. They have school band rehearsal," Vivian said, still clearing the table.

"What school stuff is on a Sunday?" I asked.

"They have a big performance next week."

"They do? Well, maybe they can skip it. It's not like I'm here that often."

"And whose fault is that?" Vivian shot back.

"Don't start with that right now, please. All I am saying is, I barely get to see them."

"So you take a solo three-hour walking tour of Manhattan?"

"I was walking the dog and getting Barney's!"

"We didn't need Barney's! The dog only needs a ten-minute walk. If you want to spend time with your family, then spend time with your family when we are here. Now the kids and I have things to do."

"Where are you going?"

"I have my hair appointment and then a manicure."

"Wow, busy day."

"The world doesn't stop and start when you come to town. Go shove that Barney bullshit up your ass, Max!"

5.

I always wore a suit when I flew. It projected class and strength to strangers. When it came to strangers, no place could outdo the airport in terms of volume and variety. Duncan was the one who insisted I wore a suit nearly everywhere I went: "My lawyer has to be dressed to kill always and everywhere!" Initially, I was self-conscious about always standing out, but people treated me with respect and dignity. After that, I was hooked. The deference I received was intoxicating.

I was *shvitzing* like Moses in the desert outside my apartment for a taxicab in ninety-nine-degree weather. It was like doing yoga in a sauna with a straightjacket wearing this suit. I had plenty of time before takeoff but preferred to get drunk at the airport over an excruciating goodbye with my wife. I felt like an unwelcome stranger in my own home.

When the taxi finally arrived, I hurried into the back seat for the air-conditioning while the driver threw my bags in the trunk. I repacked the cash designated for London throughout my clothes in my carry-on bag. I would have rather left the money in New York to avoid the risk of carrying it through airport security. For all I knew, I was already on a no-fly list in the tri-state area. Still, compared to Duncan's reaction if I failed to deliver this money, it was worth the risk. To that end, I never called Duncan back after having ignored his call last night. Better to make the call at the airport bar; his verbal lashing would be easier to handle emotionally after a couple of shots of whiskey.

"Where we headed?" the taxi driver asked.

"Newark Airport. I'm early, so don't drive like a maniac," I replied.

I was glad to leave my family shit behind in New York but, at the same time, was wary to return to San Francisco.

CHAPTER 3

Dirty Sand

San Francisco, California

1.

Frequent sunshine with rising temperatures began as soon as the summer season ended. Fortunately, the same room I'd rented at the Ocean Beach Motel was available. This shitty motel room felt more like home than the Manhattan apartment I shared with my wife and kids. Text and voice messages from Duncan littered my phone once I landed at SFO. Already in a work suit, it was easier to go directly from the airport to Duncan's office.

During the cross-country flight, I'd decided I would come clean to Duncan about my failure to deliver the payoff to London. I would omit my encounter with SFPD, however.

Inexplicably, I did not hear Duncan verbally admonishing some poor bastard who worked for him when I entered his office.

"Max, thanks for coming," he said with a huge smile.

"Of course, boss. You tell me to come, and I come," I replied.

"How is your father?" Duncan asked.

"Oh, you know, as good as an eighty-five-year-old with bad eyesight and a hearing aid can be."

"I'm sure he was happy to see his only son. And how are Vivian and the children?"

"Everyone is great, boss. I appreciate you asking about them."

"Of course. I'm happy that you're back."

Nearly a minute passed before I decided to break the silence with a confession. "Listen, boss, I have to come clean on something."

"Oh, what is it?"

"I wasn't able to deliver the money to London," I said with my head down.

"Really? Larry said you picked up the money."

"I did, yes, but when I went to London to drop it off, she wasn't home. I waited as long as I could, but she never showed up."

"I see, I see," Duncan said, stroking his chin.

"I have it, the money, I mean, if you want it back."

"You keep it. Just make sure she gets it."

"Of course. I'll try again today," I stammered, completely caught off guard by Duncan's calm and reasonable response.

"I know I can count on you, Max, for everything and anything."

"Absolutely, boss, whatever you need," I said as serious as a heart attack.

Another minute passed with Duncan just smiling without saying a word. Again, I took it upon myself to break the silence. "You wanted to see me about something, boss?"

"Yes, of course. I need you to give a friend of mine some advice," Duncan replied.

"A friend? Advice? You mean like counsel?"

"Exactly. He needs some legal help. I told him I have a very talented lawyer that is perfect for the job."

"Are you talking about me?"

"Of course I'm talking about you! You shouldn't be so humble, Max. You're the most outstanding lawyer in town."

"You are talking about me?"

"I want you to see my friend Richard Sand. He is a very talented individual, and he is in a bit of a jam. Go see him as soon as possible," Duncan ordered and handed me a piece of a paper with an address.

"Sure thing, boss. I'm on top of it," I replied enthusiastically. "What about the money for London?"

"Go to that address and see Richard first. It's very important. It needs your attention right away. After that, make sure to get the money to London."

"Consider it done."

2.

Richard Sand's house was located right next to the Tenderloin, an area that was previously filled exclusively with low-priced housing projects and drug-filled streets before it had been gentrified. As a result, instead of a couple of homeless people and drug dealers spread around several blocks, now there were just two blocks completely overrun with junkies, psychos, and criminals.

Richard Sand's place was stunningly clean. The floor was so smooth I nearly fell ass-backward when I went to shake his hand. Richard offered me a drink, and being the dutiful guest, I accepted. He brought out two huge glasses filled with a bright-blue liquid as we made our way to the living room.

"What kind of drink is that?" I asked.

"Absinthe with a bit of sugar," he replied.

"Doesn't that combination cause hallucinations?" I inquired.

"Only if prepared correctly," he replied with a grin.

I could not believe that this man was drinking, *and serving,* absinthe in the middle of the day, but I did not want to be rude and slowly sipped it and took my seat.

"Duncan told me you've worked for him for a few years now," Richard said.

"Yes, it has been my privilege to serve him as his counsel," I replied.

"Your privilege? I can see why he likes you so much," Richard smiled.

I smiled back, not sure if Richard was being complimentary or condescending.

"So what can I help you with?"

"How is Duncan's temper?" Richard asked, oblivious to my question.

"His temper? You know Duncan. He is very … passionate."

"Yes, passionate." Richard smiled again. "He has become more passionate as he gets older, I noticed."

"Well, you know how it is with powerful men," I answered.

"Yes, of course. Duncan is a great man." Richard nodded.

"Yes, a great man." I nodded in return.

"What can you help me with?" Richard asked.

"Excuse me?" I asked with a perplexed tone.

"Your earlier question, why I asked you here. I have something very important to ask you, but I need your discretion," he told me as he handed me a piece of paper with a dollar bill clipped to it.

"Is this a contract to be your lawyer?" I asked.

"And payment," Richard explained.

"For one dollar? You must think I'm a pretty shitty lawyer," I remarked.

"It's just a formality."

"Fine," I said and signed the damn piece of paper.

"Great." Richard grabbed the paper from my hand. "Don't forget your dollar."

He passed it on the freshly polished wooden table that was between us. I collected the dollar, and we both gulped down some absinthe.

"Okay, so I need representation," Richard continued.

"I thought you just needed advice?" I asked.

"Yes, your counsel. I need you to represent me in court for a misdemeanor."

"What's the charge?"

"Assault with a deadly weapon," he casually responded.

I nearly spat out my drink all over his pristinely clean carpet. "Misdemeanor assault with a deadly weapon?"

"Technically, it is a wobbler."

"It is a serious crime and a felony."

"California law states that punishment for that crime is less than one year in jail, which would mean it is a misdemeanor."

"That's one possible outcome. Another is a minimum of five years in prison."

"Exactly. It can go either way. That's why it's a wobbler."

"I would certainly say that's an optimistic view of the potential outcomes."

"I am nothing if not an optimist." Richard chuckled. This chuckle of his was quite disturbing and reminded me of how a ventriloquist dummy looked when he "laughed."

"If I were to take this case, there is no way I can do it for a dollar—"

"Pay yourself with the ten thousand dollars Duncan gave you for the other thing," Richard interrupted.

"Duncan told you about the other thing?" I asked in shock.

"No, he just told me to tell you to use the money for the other thing. I am smart enough not to discuss specifics with Duncan," Richard clarified.

"Duncan didn't mention any of this to me."

"Double-check with him if you need to. But I know what he told me. The hearing is tomorrow. I'll meet you there."

"Okay. If Duncan backs up what you are saying—"

"He will," Richard interrupted me.

"If he does, I will prepare a list of all your options."

"No jail time."

"Say again?"

"I won't accept any deal that includes jail time," Richard repeated.

"You are expecting no jail time with an assault with a deadly weapon charge?"

"I told you, I am an optimist." He chuckled (again).

"To be honest, you sound delusional," I replied. "But I'll see what I can do."

"I know you will. Duncan told me you are a very talented lawyer."

Despite his clean and polished floors, I felt filthy after talking to Richard Sand. I had done a lot of *treif* business for Duncan, but there was something particularly disturbing about Richard. Why the hell would Duncan want to help out this creep? Why insist that I be his lawyer? If Richard told me to keep the money designated to London, did that mean I didn't need to find London anymore? There had been no mention of Sarah Verand even in the slightest. For someone who watched as much television as Duncan did, it was inconceivable he was unaware of her murder. Duncan was hiding something from me. To be fair, I hadn't told him about talking to the police, so I guess we both had our secrets.

It would have been prudent to confirm the "directives" Richard gave me. But Duncan had sent me there himself, so he must've been clued in. I was so fatigued I plopped onto my small motel bed when I got back to Ocean Beach. After a couple of minutes, my lungs were unable to get enough oxygen. I picked up my phone to dial 9-1-1 as I lost consciousness.

3.

I woke up in a pool of my sweat on the unsanitary floor of my motel room. I took out my phone and saw that I'd dialed 9-1-1 but had failed to hit send. I tried to get my head straight by drinking whiskey straight from the bottle. Something was wrong—a puzzle with missing pieces. Shit-faced, I decided a walk by the beach at two in the morning seemed appropriate.

The boardwalk was windy as hell, and though it was a very dark night, I could still see the humongous waves. It was warmer the farther away I walked from the ocean. Before I knew it, an hour had passed, and I arrived at London's apartment building. My instinct nagged me that she knew something I did not—a missing piece of the puzzle.

"I might as well see if she's home," I mumbled to myself.

I incessantly rang the doorbell and banged on the door for several minutes. She might have been working, though by now, the strip clubs had been closed for over an hour. Maybe she simply was not answering the door in the middle of the night like a sensible person. I tried pulling the door handle out of frustration, but it turned without a problem. It had been unlocked the whole time. Even though the door was unlocked, waltzing in uninvited might constitute "breaking and entering," or at the very least "entering." My curiosity overcame my reluctance.

The place was a *disheveled* mess—clothes all over the place, television busted open on the floor, and furniture turned inside out. If London had been here when the place was ransacked, her life could be in major jeopardy.

I was relieved not to see her corpse in the bedroom. There was not any blood on the walls or floor in the rest of the apartment either. It was unlikely London had been around when her apartment was being torn to shreds.

Did she know she was in trouble? And what the hell were these people looking for in the first place?

I wiped the door handle twice before closing the door. Luckily, there were no nosy neighbors in the hallway. I exited the building and traveled a mile toward my motel before I stopped to gain my senses, along with my breath. I suddenly became paranoid that someone had seen me enter London's apartment. What had compelled me to check her place out? If I didn't know better, it was almost like I was trying to get caught.

Something smelled rotten, and I couldn't help but think that Duncan was somehow responsible for the stench. As a lawyer, though, ignorance was not only bliss but also legally responsible. Yet for some reason, I was compelled not to let sleeping dogs lie. Already implicated in Sarah's murder, I had somehow got myself mixed up in whatever was happening with London as well. Regardless, I had to get ready for court in mere hours. Whatever crisis London was going through would have to wait until I was finished with this Richard Sand *meshugas*.

4.

On my way to court, I pondered whether representing this creep Richard Sand was a type of punishment. It certainly felt that way. That sentiment was reinforced when I arrived at the courthouse and saw Richard in a ridiculous purple suit with a purple top hat.

"Did you purposefully dress up as a comic book villain?" I asked.

"What can I say? I dress to impress," Richard replied. "Ready to win this thing?"

"I barely know anything about it, but sure, why not?" I impatiently replied.

"Don't worry. It's in the bag," Richard said, patting me (too hard) on the back.

"How is that?" I asked with raised eyebrows.

"Trust me. It's taken care of. I am going to plead not guilty, and all you have to say is the case should be dismissed," he assured me.

"Why would the judge dismiss the case out of hand like that?"

"Because the prosecution doesn't have a witness."

"You mean the guy you assaulted?"

"Don't worry about it. It is all taken care of." Richard chuckled again.

"Listen, if you did anything to tamper with this case or intimidated a witness—"

"Whatever I did was with the advisory of counsel," Richard interrupted me.

"Are you talking about me?"

"You're my lawyer, aren't you?" Richard chuckled yet again.

"You chuckle one more time, and I will advise you to block my fist from your nose."

"We better get to court," Richard said without even a smile.

* * *

The three days it took for a verdict felt like a year had passed. Richard's prediction bore out correct; he was given community service, no jail time. The man who was "allegedly" assaulted did not show up to court. Nor could he be reached by phone, email, or even a physical visit by an officer of the court. The guy disappeared, and consequently, so did the case against Richard. The judge was so upset she still gave him community service, regardless of the lack of evidence. Richard wanted to fight it, but I explained to him that would piss off the court and prosecutors, which could lead to an investigation, with severe consequences *if* Richard had something to do with the disappearance of the victim. Richard reluctantly accepted the judge's sentence.

Since then, things had settled down. Duncan was pleased with the job I had done. The police had not questioned me about Sarah Verand since I'd spoken with Chief Willard Williams. There was still no sign from London, but this mess was in my rear view, and I'd even come up $10,000. However, the stress had been too much. It was time to do something different with my life. If that meant not working for Duncan anymore, then I had to start preparing for that reality. I needed to heed the advice of my father and move back to New York and invest in my family instead of my career.

The sun was shining, and the weather was unusually hot, an actual San Francisco beach day. I took a few hotel hand towels and laid myself out near the ocean water. I stared at the bright blue sky while enjoying the refreshing breeze that gently massaged my face. For the first time in a long time, I was truly grateful to be alive. A great weight had been lifted from my shoulders.

I returned to my room at ease. I had closed my eyes for an afternoon nap when suddenly there was a loud knock on my door. I initially ignored it, but the knocking persisted, gradually becoming louder and louder.

My jaw dropped in shock when I finally answered the door. "What are you doing here, London?"

"Duncan is trying to kill me, just like he killed Sarah!"

PART II

The Mess

Chapter 4

All In

Las Vegas, Nevada

1.

London was likely inebriated at the blackjack table, losing hundreds of dollars. The ten grand originally meant for London to keep quiet about her affair with Duncan was already significantly reduced since our arrival in Vegas a couple of days before. I was unable to pay for anything with my credit or debit cards, including the hotel, to avoid electronic footprints that Duncan (or the police) could follow to our location. As a further precaution, I told my wife I was in Los Angeles on business, in case anyone contacted her about my whereabouts. It was not like she had any intention to call me, regardless of my geographical location. We even checked into the hotel with a driver's license with the name of one of London's aliases, Sunshine. I did not inquire why London carried several drivers' licenses on her, all from different states with different names, but I was sure a stripper who had affairs with billionaires had her reasons.

London was convinced Duncan had ordered some goon to kill her. I told her to go to the police, but she said the person who was after her was a cop who went by Sergeant Tolliver. It didn't help matters that the police considered me a person of interest in the Sarah Verand murder.

Between the hit man and the police, we needed to get out of the Bay Area immediately. Fortunately, we were able to get the first available flight to Las Vegas. Why did I choose Las Vegas as a hideout? For one, it was out of the jurisdiction of the SFPD's and Chief Willard Williams's grasp. Second, London had lived there before and told me she had reliable connections if we needed help. Lastly, Las Vegas was ideal to carry around $10,000 in a briefcase without being conspicuous.

I needed to buy time to come up with a plan to fix this *farkakte* situation. If Duncan was conducting "funny business" without telling me, I was in more jeopardy than I imagined. The biggest question mark was how Sarah Verand had found out about his and London's affair in the first place. That was a massive missing piece to this sordid puzzle.

Not helping matters was London's vow of silence on everything Duncan. Speaking of which, I needed to find her. She had been gone all day, and on her own, she was a liability. Besides, it was a good excuse to do something besides getting high and drunk while watching cable news. We were staying at a fairly new hotel mid-Strip near the Statue of Liberty and Eiffel Tower. I made my way through several hotel casinos in a daze of stress, weed, and hard liquor looking for London, but there was no sign of her. I required a break and plopped myself at a blackjack table to rest for a moment.

"Are you playing, sir?" a middle-aged male dealer with a clean haircut inquired.

"I am just resting for a second," I replied.

"Sorry, sir, seats are for players only."

"No one else is sitting here."

"Seats are for players only," the dealer repeated.

"Fine, what type of game is it anyway?"

"Free bet blackjack." The dealer smiled.

"What's free about it?"

"You can double on 9, 10, and 11 for free, but you can only hit one time after that."

"Like a double-or-nothing thing?" I asked.

"Not exactly, but it does make the bet more attractive," the dealer said and took my hundred dollar bill and exchanged it for five twenty-dollar chips. He dealt me a five of hearts and six of spades. The dealer was showing a nine of hearts.

"What the hell, it's free, right? Double that sucker," I said with enthusiasm.

"Exactly right, sir," the dealer replied and dealt me a seven of clubs. The dealer turned over his blind card and showed a queen of hearts.

"Nineteen beats eighteen," the dealer said and mercilessly collected my chips into his hidden pile.

"One more." I bet the rest of my chips. I got eight of diamonds and a two of clubs. He was only showing a seven of spade.

"Double that!" I yelled. I received a shitty seven of hearts. He turned over an ace of spade.

"Eighteen beats seventeen. House wins," the dealer said, collecting my last stack.

"For something that is free, it sure costs a lot," I noted as I left the table.

I shook my head in disgust. I knew better than to think anything was free. When making a bet, be prepared to lose everything.

2.

London was topless watching television on the bed in the hotel room when I came back.

"What the hell are you doing?" I asked.

"What does it look like? I'm watching TV," she replied.

"I was looking for you all over the Las Vegas Strip!" I yelled.

"I met that friend I was talking to you about," she replied.

"For four hours?"

"And I had a couple of drinks, placed a couple of bets—"

"Do you really think that is the best thing to do right now?"

"Drinking and gambling in Las Vegas? Yeah, that's why people come here."

"You seem pretty relaxed for someone who has a murder contract on her head."

"It's been a stressful week. I am just trying to remain calm. You should try it. Why the hell are you so uptight anyway?"

"I am on the lam because you asked for my help. So if you don't mind, keep me aware of where you are at all times. We are in this together, at least until I can reach Duncan and sort out this mess."

"Duncan? Are you crazy? He is responsible for all of this."

"You don't know that."

"He killed Sarah!"

"You don't know that!" I repeated. "Regardless, without any evidence, there is no way to prove it. If we just make allegations without backing it up, we will just get into deeper shit."

"Sarah Verand's murder is all over the news. You're probably a suspect, and Duncan is trying to kill me to keep my mouth shut. I would say we hit bottom."

"It can always get worse, trust me. We need a plan before we do anything else, something that we are in control of and execute successfully."

"Okay," London said as she turned off the television, "what's your plan?"

"First thing is you need to tell me everything," I replied.

"I told you everything already!" London responded defensively.

"Bullshit! You're not telling me the whole story." I indignantly pointed my finger in her direction. I took a breath and poured myself a large glass of whiskey and one for her. "Tell me what I need to know."

"Okay, fine. What do you want to know exactly?"

"Who told Sarah about you and Duncan's affair?"

"I can't tell you that."

Exasperated, I drank the whole whiskey glass and asked, "Why won't you tell me who you are protecting?"

"Because I am in love with him," London said, on the verge of tears.

"You are in love with Duncan?"

"Not Duncan! He is a disgusting bully with a small dick!"

"Okay. Small dicks aside, the only people, to my knowledge, aware of your affair are Duncan, you, and me. I know I didn't say anything. And you say you didn't say anything. And if Duncan is trying so hard to keep the affair quiet, then certainly he didn't say anything. Taking that all into account, that means somebody else said something, which means that somebody else knew—presumably the person you are protecting. Duncan didn't tell me about this person either, which is odd because confronting this unknown person should be my job. Okay, so the both of you are protecting the same person," I said, thinking aloud to London.

"What the hell are you talking about?"

"Who would you both be protecting?" I continued. "Obviously, somebody close to Duncan but also somebody you say you love—"

"I do love him!" London interrupted me.

"The only people Duncan would stick his neck out for would be his family."

"It doesn't matter who it is!"

"The hell it doesn't," I snapped back. "Who would you screw in Duncan's family?"

"How dare you!"

"It can't be his deceased father, and I am certain his wife and his daughters wouldn't be involved in something like that, with you at least—"

"What the hell is that supposed to mean?"

"No way is it his brother."

"Why can't it be Duncan's brother?"

"Because he's gay."

"Okay. That is a good reason."

"That just leaves Junior. Holy shit. This is bad—very, very bad."

"You can't tell anybody!"

"Just be straight with me, okay? Did you have an affair with Junior before or after your affair with Duncan?"

London turned away from me again and solemnly replied, "Before."

"Damn it! This is all about Junior. But why cut me out, unless …"

"Unless what?" London inquired.

"Unless I am somehow the fall guy."

"Then we are both fucked."

3.

For a man who was supposed to know everything regarding Duncan, it turned out I was the man who knew too little. The realization that I was in over my head hit me like a ton of bricks. Duncan would go to extreme lengths to protect his eldest son. Not only was he family and the heir to his kingdom, but he also had Duncan's name. He would not suffer the embarrassment of having had an affair with the same woman as his son. If Sarah had known about London and Junior, Duncan would have been desperate to prevent it from becoming public. If it was a choice between his eldest son taking the fall or me, it was really no choice at all. London was right; I was fucked.

Depressed, anxious, and shvitzing all over the place, I required urgent relief; I drank and vaped myself into an incoherent stupor. Delirious, I dreamed of potential outcomes to my dire situation. First, I had a horrifying vision of Bubba, an obese, bald-headed, pig-nosed man missing his two front teeth with whom I shared my prison cell. Next, I was lying on the floor in a pool of my own blood, dying a painful and lonely death. Then I saw myself with my wife, kids, father, and even Zevi, laughing and smiling together, enraptured in love. My last dream was of a sunny day on a white-sand beach in front of a transparent blue ocean and a gentle breeze massaging my face.

When I awoke in my hotel, London was nowhere to be seen. Should I just give up and let the cards land as they fell? Being in Las Vegas, it was an appropriate analogy. Following the urge to spend the rest of the cash in the briefcase and see where the Las Vegas night would take me felt extremely easy, and shit had been so damn hard lately. The idea became more appealing as another bottle of whiskey became emptier. I took a couple thousand dollars in cash and went out to the abyss that was a Las Vegas night.

Stumbling out of the elevator to the casino floor, I made my way to another blackjack table. Several free drinks later, I was already down $500. I bought several packs of cigarettes, a calamitous turn since I had not smoked a single cigarette in nearly twenty years. I proceeded to play at a craps table with a whiskey soda and a cigarette dancing out of my mouth. I continually yelled at some old man in a nice buttoned shirt, "Let's go, shooter!"

He humored me initially, but after several minutes of me yelling at him, he began to get angry. When I told him, "You better not fuck me on this shot, old yeller!" he threw the dice at my head and nailed me in the forehead. I barely even noticed.

After I lost my third bet in a row, I began yelling, "You fucked me, girl!" to a woman in her sixties from Oklahoma.

The dealer finally called security, and I was removed from the casino. It was just as well because, in that short amount of time, I'd lost nearly all the money I had on me. I decided to go all in and spend the rest of my money at a strip club. I still had roughly $300 left, which was enough cash for a good time.

I sought out a street promoter and negotiated limo service to the Pink Giraffe, a higher-end strip club. I even got him to throw in a fifth of Courvoisier and a pack of cigarettes for $100. Before I knew it, the promoter was holding the door open to the limo. There was a young couple already in the back. I could only imagine what they thought of me—a man in his late forties wearing a completely disheveled Italian suit stinking of booze and cigarettes taking a limo to a strip club at three in the morning. I was a classic Las Vegas midlife crisis.

"Hey there, fellah," the boyfriend said with a thick Irish accent. "Fun night?" He wore a funny brown fedora on his shaved head.

"It's been okay," I replied, looking for a lighter.

"Well, it should get a whole lot better where we're going," he said, handing me his lighter. "Mind if I and the missus have one?"

I threw him the pack, and he put two cigarettes in his mouth and lit both of them and handed one to his female companion.

"Thanks a million."

"No problem," I said.

A minute later, the limo was a thick cloud of secondhand tobacco smoke. I opened the complimentary bottle of Courvoisier and began chugging it.

"Where you guys from?" I asked after passing the bottle over to my fellow passengers, who joyfully took their own respective chugs.

The man handed me back the bottle. "Dublin."

"What brings you all the way here?"

"First time in America. We, well, could not leave without checking out Sin City," the man replied.

The woman began laughing uncontrollably before she suddenly collapsed onto her male partner's lap.

"Is she okay?" I asked him.

"What? Her? Oh, sure." He chuckled. "She is just taking a wee nap."

"What else have you seen?"

"Today we went to the Hoo-oo-ver Dam. Hotter than fuck it was. We saw Los Angeles, Hollywo-ood, California," the Irishman replied.

I mentioned I was living in San Francisco while we both smoked another cigarette.

"Oh, wow, we loved it there. That place is a blast!"

"Even with all of the fog?"

"Are you kidding? Compared to Ireland, that weather is a breeze from the wings of an angel."

"To tell you the truth, I am thinking of leaving," I continued.

"Why?" he asked.

"My boss is a real asshole."

"Can't you quit?"

"I am in a bit of a complicated legal situation."

"You should get a lawyer."

"I am a lawyer."

"That's hilarious." He laughed. "You seem way too tense, friend. Take one of these." He handed me a white pill with an imprint of a rabbit. "This here is pure MDMA. Swallow that, and your problems will be gone. I promise you that."

The Irishman's argument was quite convincing. We both took a pill with a swig of the Courvoisier. We arrived at the Pink Giraffe a minute later.

When the driver opened the door, the woman popped back up and screamed, "I'm ready to see some tits!"

4.

A topless hostess walked me over to an empty table and, soon after, brought me a double of Irish whiskey. Strippers continually asked me if I wanted a private dance. Regrettably, I had to be sparse with the remaining money I had and politely refused. I was staring at the performances being conducted on several of the "stages" when a new girl began working the pole on the main stage. Despite not being able to clearly see her face, something rang familiar about her breasts. *Holy shit, that's London!*

I was so fucked up I could not be absolutely sure if it was actually London or if I was hallucinating from the MDMA. I blundered closer to the stage for confirmation.

"London! London!" I yelled to her from the stage floor.

Recognizing me, she shook her head in disbelief. After sticking a customer between her breasts, she came over to my side of the stage. "What the hell are you doing here?" she asked.

"I was going to ask you the same thing," I replied.

"What does it look like? I'm working!" she told me as she stuffed my head in the middle of her breasts.

"Do you really think this is a good idea?" I asked her when I was able to breathe again.

"Why not?"

"It's not exactly maintaining a low profile."

"I go by a different name here, okay? If you want to continue talking, you need to buy yourself a private dance."

"With you? God, no."

"Fuck you, Max." London strutted off the stage.

"Where the hell are you going?"

I tried following her to the other end of the stage but was intercepted by a big and bulky man.

"Plenty of other girls here tonight, fella," the bouncer firmly informed me.

"I need to talk with that one over there," I hurriedly replied.

"I think the lady made her feelings known to you," he said with his hand firmly on my chest, physically stopping me.

"I get that. I just need—"

"You just need to go to the other end of this establishment or exit peacefully," he told me before roughly turning and pushing me in the other direction.

I was keen on keeping an eye on London. There were worse places to wait than a strip club, so I decided to stay for London's shift to end. Several drinks and a pack of cigarettes passed before I realized I had not seen London for nearly an hour. I started going around the club frantically looking for her. Suddenly, the bouncer I'd encountered before swung me around and asked what I was doing.

"Yeah, that girl from earlier—"

"Still hung up on her, I see." The guard stared me down.

"No, I am not … whatever, have you seen her?" I asked.

"Sorry, buddy. She left already."

"Was she with anyone?"

"Don't get hung up on her. Plenty of other girls here, fella—"

I darted out of the club before he finished his sentence. London was nowhere to be seen. I took a cab back to the hotel. The hotel room was completely empty. London was gone.

5.

The hotel mattress was soaked when I awoke the next morning, in what I hoped was only sweat. My throat felt like I had just swallowed fire, so I rushed to the bathroom sink faucet and drank as much water as I could.

I then proceeded to vomit for several minutes while I showered. While I dried myself with a used towel from the day before, I remembered London had disappeared. I quickly stuffed all my things in my small suitcase and briefcase and dumped everything else into the garbage. Despite leaving town without knowing London's whereabouts, an early checkout from the room, and Las Vegas, was the prudent thing to do.

To begin with, it was not like London was a trustworthy person. There was a strong likelihood she'd taken some money and headed out of town as quickly as possible, an example I would be wise to follow. Of course, I could not help but consider the dreadful possibility that one of Duncan's henchmen had kidnapped her and that she'd ended up like Sarah Verand.

I spent nearly the rest of my cash on a French coffee and croissant at Hotel France and smoked my last cigarette. Throwing down the matchbox on the table, I read Pink Giraffe on the cover with the address and a number for the "establishment" on the back. It couldn't hurt to double back to the strip club on the way to the airport to check if anyone had seen London leave last night, and with whom.

The bouncer I'd encountered last night greeted me outside the Pink Giraffe's entrance. "You sure came back quickly." He grimaced.

"Yeah, I wanted to ask about one of the girls—"

"You're still hung up on her?"

"Not exactly," I stammered. "I just need to know where she is right now."

"Sorry, pal, but once those women exit the premises, you can no longer interact with them any further. Strict policy in these parts."

"It's not like that. She is a friend of mine, and I am concerned about her."

"I am sure you are really concerned, pal," he replied condescendingly.

I could see that this conversation did not have much of a future. "I just want to know what happened to her. She's a friend of mine."

"Sure, a friend. I bet you two are friends, huh, pal?" He giggled.

"You said once the girls here leave the premises the customers aren't allowed to interact with them, right?"

"Strict policy. Once the performers exit the premises, the customers can no longer interact with them further."

"I know. I just said that." I shook my head. "Listen, if you have the strict policy in place—"

"Strict policy. Once the women leave the premises—"

"Oh, for fuck's sake!" I screamed. "If no one can interact with them, how did she end up leaving with a customer?"

"Who? Jimmy? Jimmy was her handler," the man replied.

"Is that who she left with?"

"All the girls leave the premises with Jimmy. He walks them to their cars. He sometimes even gives them rides home."

"Where can I find this Jimmy?"

"His shift starts in an hour or so. But if she exited the premises, I should remind you …"

6.

While waiting to confront this Jimmy fella, I reflected on my "all in" night. It had been neither cathartic nor enjoyable. Now I just had less money and more trouble. There was no escaping my problems. No amount of drugs, gambling, and topless woman were going to get me out of this dire mess. The only way to get past this was to face this situation head-on. A good first step would be to find London.

The physical urge to smoke cigarettes and drink whiskey while waiting was incredibly strong, but I successfully resisted the temptation. If surrendering to my desires last night was a mistake, then the opposite must be right. A calm mind, body, and soul could be what were required at this time to take some control of my destiny.

A short bald man with a tight shirt and athletic sweatpants entered the complex with a shit-smiling grin. My bouncer "friend" signaled with his large head that was the Jimmy I was waiting for. I attempted to introduce myself, but Jimmy walked right past me without the slightest acknowledgment of my existence. Between my newfound sobriety and the unrelenting hangover, I was in a rotten mood and grabbed him by the arm with all my might.

"Who the hell are you?" Jimmy asked. He tightened his free hand into a fist, ready to brawl.

"I'm the guy who needs to ask you a few questions," I replied, still holding his arm tight.

"Jimmy doesn't answer to nobody!" Jimmy barked.

Caught off guard by Jimmy speaking in the third person, I let go of him. "I just want to ask about a girl who was working here last night," I tried to reassure him and took a step back.

Jimmy relaxed his fist and shoulders, fashioning a gentler demeanor. "Which broad you fall in love with?" Jimmy asked.

"London."

"I don't know any London." Jimmy shrugged and began to walk away.

"She isn't a local dancer," I chirped. "She just came in last night from out of town."

"Oh yeah, we had a newbie here last night. She was a peculiar broad, but it was obvious she knew her way around a pole. But she told us her name was Sunny or something," Jimmy responded.

"Sunshine," I replied.

"Yeah, Sunshine. I don't know much about her."

"What happened after her set?"

"All I did was walk her to her car, and they drove off," Jimmy said like he'd rehearsed the line before.

"They? Who were they?"

"Some driver was waiting for her when she was done. Asked me to walk her over."

"And you just put her in a car because some John asks?"

"What are you trying to say?" Jimmy asked defensively.

"Where the hell is she?"

"Listen, buddy, I just put her in a car."

"You tell me who paid you to put her in that car, or I'll call the police and make sure there is holy hell to pay."

"Police? Listen, I just work here on the weekends. I am not some tough-guy mobster. I was never handed any money!"

"I said stop bullshitting me already!"

"There was no handoff. They wired it to me with some Bitcoin app on my phone," Jimmy stammered.

"You mean internet money?"

"Well, actually, it's real money."

"Just tell me how much they paid you."

"It came out to roughly $3,000."

"A measly three grand to kill a broad?"

"What the hell? He just told me to put her in a car to meet some guy. No one said anything about killing nobody."

"What guy?"

"I don't know, some rich guy, a VIP. I was sent a picture of some random stripper and that if she was to come here, I needed to call him,"

Jimmy said with a pubescent tweak in his voice. "He told me to accompany her to some car that was already outside after her shift."

"What is his name?"

"The rich VIP, no idea."

"The guy who called you and wired you the money!"

"Larry!"

"Are you sure the guy's name was Larry? Fuck me," I mumbled under my breath. "Tell me the description of the car. You better give me that guy's number."

"Do you think something bad happened to her?" Jimmy asked sincerely.

"For both our sakes, I fucking hope not."

CHAPTER 5

The Smart Bet

San Francisco, California

1.

The smart bet was that London was stashed away in some Las Vegas hotel room or killed in the same manner as Sarah Verand. However, in Las Vegas, even the smart bet seldom won. I would like to believe Duncan liked London too much to kill her. Regardless, staying in Las Vegas could only do me more harm. I headed back to San Francisco without London and with my tail between my legs.

After the seat belt sign turned off during my return flight, I bought a double whiskey and poured it over a singular ice cube in a plastic cup while figuring out what the hell was happening. At this point, Duncan's complicity in capturing London was beyond a reasonable doubt. Larry would not even call his mother without Duncan knowing about it. If Larry was involved, that inherently meant Duncan was involved as well. If Duncan was mixed up in kidnapping London, did that implicate him in the murder of Sarah Verand? After finishing my whiskey, I took another sobriety pledge: *Okay. Being sober starting now!*

More of a concern than Duncan's involvement was my own. The SFPD possessed a tape of me directly threatening Sarah right before she was found dead in a parking lot. Then London and I went on the lam to Las Vegas, only for me to lose her to Duncan's own thugs. More and more, this meshugas was finding its way onto my doorstep. The more I got involved, the more likely a suspect I became.

I was stuck between a rock and a hard place. The rock—I needed to talk to Duncan to figure out what to do next. The hard place—I needed to keep as much distance as possible between me and Duncan. If Duncan ordered the murder of Sarah without telling me, it meant he didn't want me to know for a reason. Almost for certain, it was not for my protection.

The only bit of information I had to use was Duncan Jr.'s affair with London. I needed to find out if his father knew and when he knew it. Unfortunately, right as I was in a car to see Junior, I received a call from Richard Sand. I had no idea what he wanted, but I knew it was not going to be good news.

"What do you want?" I asked impatiently.

"Is that how you talk to one of your favorite clients?" I could hear his smirk through the phone in his reply.

"I only have two clients, and you're my third favorite," I replied.

"Listen, I want to talk about my case," Richard said.

"Go ahead and talk."

"No, no. We must talk in person."

"Okay. When?"

"Now is good."

"Now? I can't do now. I'm on my way to something."

"Why don't you come now, and we can talk about your trip to England."

"I wasn't in England."

"Oh, really? I heard you took a tour of *London*."

Though confusing, I could tell London was innuendo for the person and not the city. "I am coming by. It will be nice to chat with you."

"Great, I will see—"

I hung up the phone before Richard finished his sentence.

"Driver, I need to go somewhere else," I yelled.

"You must put in the new address on the app, sir," he replied.

"I'll tell you where I need to go, and you can put it in."

"You must put in the new address on the app, sir," the driver repeated.

It took me two minutes to send Richard Sand's address to the driver a foot away from me.

2.

I nearly slipped and fell entering Richard Sand's place.

"What the hell is the matter with your floor?" I asked.

"There is absolutely nothing wrong with my floor," he replied.

"It's so slippery Tonya Harding is going to skate right by me."

"Oh, I wax it every day," he casually remarked.

"Why the hell would you do that?"

"In case I drop anything, it will be clean enough to eat," he said.

"It looks like you just cleaned up after a bloody murder," I replied as we made our way to the living room, which, thankfully, had a carpet I could stand on.

"You can never be too careful, right?" Richard responded with his smirk.

It was impossible to tell if he was joking or not.

"What do you have to say about London?" I asked.

"I thought I told you I wanted to talk about the case," Richard replied, again with a smirk.

"It's always something twisted with you, isn't it, Dick?" I replied with a smirk of my own. If Richard wanted a smirk war, he would get one today.

"I prefer Richard," he replied, this time sans smirk.

"Whatever you say, Dick."

"I have to inform you that I, for the record, was not okay with how you handled my case. It made me very uncomfortable."

"What the hell are you talking about? I barely did anything on the case," I replied in exasperation.

"You were my lawyer for my wobbler, correct?"

"I represented you on your assault with a weapon charge, if that is the wobbler you are referring to."

"Precisely, and you told me to intimidate the witness and victim not to come forth."

"I did what now?"

"You intimidated the witness, just like you did with Sarah Verand."

"What do you know about Sarah?"

"Duncan referred you to be my lawyer. He said you're a fixer—that you would go to whatever lengths to take care of it."

"Listen, Dick"—I leaned forward and stared directly into his snake eyes—"I have no idea what you are going on about. I didn't intimidate anyone on your behalf, and I suggest you get another lawyer for the inevitable future charges that will be brought against you."

"Okay, Max, if you don't want to admit it to me—"

"You wearing a wire?" I interrupted Richard.

"What? A wire? Don't be ridiculous."

"Are you recording this conversation?"

"Regardless, if I was, since you just declared that you are no longer my lawyer, this conversation would not be privileged, so you admitting you intimidated the witness and victim in my trial—"

"You filthy son of a bitch!" I stormed off.

"Before you go, I never asked you about your London trip," Richard said with his smirk returning in full force.

"What about it?"

"I heard you took her to Las Vegas to extort Duncan for money and to convince her to testify you were not involved in the murder of Sarah Verand."

"I wasn't involved."

"Anyway, that's what I heard."

"Bullshit!"

"We'll be in touch!" Richard said as I slammed the door behind me. No wonder Richard cleaned his floors every day—he was one Dirty Dick.

3.

Richard's message was received loud and clear. Richard had set me up to blackmail me into submitting to Duncan's will when the time came. By the aggressive and outlandish demeanor Richard Sand had just exhibited, I calculated that time was rapidly approaching. Not only that, Richard, in his villainous way, had communicated that London had made a deal with Duncan to implicate me as the fall guy for the murder of Sarah Verand. I'd always been aware that Duncan could turn on me, just never so damn fast. He wanted me to take the blame to protect someone he deemed more important than myself. There were only two things he would want to protect more than his business—his name and family. Luckily for Duncan Jr., he was the only person who could check both of those boxes.

Now that London had turned on me, my only option was to leverage my knowledge of Junior and London's affair. I had to get in touch with

Junior, though this would be nearly impossible, since Duncan likely had him stashed in his hotel, protected by his personal security detail. I would be thrown out and arrested before I even came close to the sliding doors.

Turning myself in to the police and ratting on Duncan was on the table. But then I would be going face-to-face against a ruthless, clever, unrelenting sociopath in a battle of wills. Knowing Duncan, he already had several witnesses and alibis ready to go to bat for Junior and himself. I was already implicated in several crimes with the actual facts of the case, let alone what Duncan would make up with fake corroborating evidence against me.

If I went home to my family, I would be putting them in danger. It was determined—neither going home nor turning myself in was an option.

Back at my motel, I changed into more comfortable, and inconspicuous, clothing. I threw everything worth anything into a bag and left the rest in the room. I stayed strong and trashed a half-drunk bottle of whiskey with my vaporizer and darted toward the beach. When I felt comfortable no one could see me in the fog and darkness, I finally allowed myself to rest.

After around ten minutes of shivering uncontrollably, a name bolted into my head—Larry! He knew everything about this crime—the payoffs, the players, and Duncan's involvement, even my role as the patsy! He was the key I needed to unlock the solution.

Larry's house was too risky for a meeting place. I needed a good reason that would both draw him out to talk to me and convince him to withhold the meeting from Duncan. There must be something on Larry I could use—a crime he'd committed on behalf of Duncan or, alternatively, an action he'd secretly had against Duncan. What leverage could there be against the cleanest and most ethical crook?

If I couldn't get anything on Larry, I would have to leverage someone close to him. I preferred not to get a person's family involved when I "convinced" someone to align with my interests, but this was a desperate situation. Honestly, it was a tactic I had used many times previously working for Duncan. Though my "fixer" abilities had gotten me into this mess, I would need to rely on them to finagle my way out.

Larry wanted to be perceived as wealthy despite not having any money. It never added up that such a good accountant was always living beyond his means. Where was his loot from working with Duncan for so long? I suppose I could look in the mirror to answer that question. I had been a higher-up employee of Duncan's "empire" for a decade and barely could put two shekels together. Come to think of it, no one who worked for Duncan had become rich. In fact, it was quite the opposite—everyone working for him was broke. Duncan was nearly broke himself and living off borrowed credit from banks so shady they were closer to loan sharks than respectable financial institutions.

Along those lines, a potential vulnerability ripe for exploitation was the pricey Jewish day school Larry sent his children to. I once checked it out for my own kids, in case we all moved out to California. The school cost thirty-five grand a year! What the hell could they possibly teach second-grade students that could be worth that much? For 35K, my six-year-old should finish calculus by the time he graduated first grade.

Regardless, Larry sent his three kids to that school, for the social status more than the quality of the education. It was only going to get more expensive when his kids went to high school and then exponentially more for the top-tier universities. If I could help him with the school, he might return the favor by helping me go against Duncan. If that was the carrot, I still needed a stick. I could investigate how he could afford the school without the means to pay for it. Maybe he was skimming from Duncan or working some loan scheme with a foreign bank.

It was too cold to sit at the beach any longer. I had some idea of what to do. At present, I needed a safe place that I could lay low. Before I fully got up, I knew exactly where to go and what favor to cash in.

4.

I scoped the surrounding area three times before I entered the Park Merced Apartment London resided in. If she were home, hopefully without any of Duncan's thugs accompanying her, I could attempt to reason with her—that was if I could keep my temper over her betrayal and conspiring in framing me for murder. My plan mainly consisted of trying to guilt-trip her into helping me, a skill I'd astutely picked up from my own mother. If London were not home, I would be shit out of luck. Both were not ideal options, but nothing had been ideal for a long time now.

I lightly knocked on London's door, careful not to be heard at this late hour. For the next two minutes, the strength of my knock gradually increased until I was banging on the damn thing. With a heavy sigh, I garnered all my strength and attempted to break the door open with my shoulder. After several attempts, I feared I was making too much noise and that my shoulder was broken. I geared up and launched myself forward for my biggest attempt yet when the door swung open right before I made contact, and I flew into London's apartment, landing on her wooden floor with a violent thud. I cringed and looked up to see London in a small bathrobe with a handgun straight in my face.

"What the hell do you think you're doing?" she asked. Her hands were visibly shaking while holding the gun at my forehead.

"I tried knocking first." I groaned writhing on the floor. "I think I broke my shoulder."

"It serves you right. I should shoot you this instant for trying to break in."

"Is that thing even loaded?"

"Do you want to find out?" she said, lowering the gun closer to my face.

"Not really," I replied.

"You make any sudden movements, and I guarantee you will," she said, moving backward, still pointing the gun in my direction.

"I'm not capable of making any sudden movements," I replied. I managed to slowly get into an upright sitting position.

"You are fucking crazy to come here."

"Not crazy, desperate. In fact, I remember you similarly coming to my door. I also remember helping you in that situation and that you repaid me by setting me up for a crime I didn't commit."

"Well," London responded and then put down the gun, "I didn't have much choice in the matter. Anyway, it's not like you had nothing to do with it."

"What the hell did I do?"

"You're Duncan's thug! You know what you've done for him!"

"Sounds like you are justifying stabbing me in the back."

"Oh, cry me a river!" London hollered and closed the door behind me.

"Okay, I get why you did what you did. I'm not saying you were even wrong to make that choice. But why help Duncan after all the terrifying shit he put you through?"

"Because he's dangerous and terrifying. Between getting killed and making $100,000 to help frame you, well, that is no choice at all—especially when you're such an asshole."

"You're right. I am an asshole. But Duncan is a considerably bigger asshole. He keeps pitting us against each other. And for what? So he can sleep with his son's stripper girlfriend? No offense, of course."

"Fuck you, Max! For all I know, you ordered Sarah's murder."

"Fair enough, but I'm telling you I didn't. Why would I do that and help you get out of town when you came to me for help? And even if you actually thought I was capable of such a monstrosity, it would only be on behalf of Duncan, and you know that is true."

"I don't give a shit about all this. I have already accepted the money, and I am not going to confront Duncan to help you. Sorry, Max, but you're going down for this, whether you killed Sarah or not."

"I told you. I had nothing to do with it!"

"Maybe so," London said, opening the front door for me to leave. "But you're no innocent, Max. Maybe you had nothing to do with it this time, but there's plenty you got away with that you sure as hell are guilty of. I don't care why you go to prison. You deserve it any way it comes."

5.

I was bruised, battered, and without a pot to piss in. At any moment, Chief Willard Williams could locate and arrest me for murder. My boss, mentor, and center of my life for the last decade had betrayed me as soon as it was convenient. I was estranged from my family to the point where Zevi was the only member of the family that liked me, and even his embrace was fairly muted for a dog. All I'd sacrificed working for Duncan was worth less than nothing; it was a curse to my damnation. Why hadn't I listened to my father? Why had I chosen Duncan over everything else? Was it the high praise he'd lavished on me? The "high life" I'd gotten only a mere taste of? The power it enabled me to have over weak and compromised people? *What the hell was I thinking?* London was right—I deserved whatever was coming to me.

Fortunately, I didn't have the benefit of time for self-pity. I had to get to Larry straightaway. He was my last prospect to avoid being completely fucked. Larry knew everything about anything Duncan related. In this particularly shitty situation, he was henchman number one. It made sense that Duncan would turn to Larry if he did not want to use my set of "skills." Considering how famous and powerful Duncan was, he only had a handful of friends and even fewer people he could trust. Those whom he did trust were never on the up-and-up—myself included.

I arrived at Larry's kids' Jewish day school early in the morning. I wanted to persuade the administration to give Larry's kids a deduction on their tuition, which I knew Larry could barely afford. It wasn't the biggest of carrots, but it was a whole lot better than the stick—get one or all of his children expelled from the school. Larry's ego could simply not afford such devastation to his social standing. I would need to string the needle to be able to present a "this or else" situation when I eventually asked Larry to help me. How I was going to accomplish one, let alone all those things, was a tall order. When life gives you rotten lemons, make disgusting lemonade and try and sell it for full price.

The campus was located at the southwestern tip of San Francisco, less than a mile from London's apartment building. Fortunately, a branch of my gym club I was a member of was nearby, so I could shower and change into my suit. Having already checked out the school two years ago, I had a natural reason to show up there unexpectedly. Any parent able to afford to pay $35,000 a year for elementary school could always get an impromptu meeting with the head of school.

Being a Jewish day school, the institution had an abundant presence of security—and with good reason with the rampant anti-Semitism in today's American culture. A man wearing a name tag that read "Trey" asked politely what business I had at the school.

"I am a prospective parent. I am in the middle of trying to move my kids here from New York," I replied.

"Okay. Check in with the office manager inside. Why do you want to move?" he asked out of curiosity.

"I work out here, but my family still lives in New York."

"Oh. Who do you work for?"

"I'm a lawyer working at Duncan Hotels."

"You know Duncan Thomas?"

"I am his personal lawyer actually," I replied.

"Okay, Mr. Duncan Thomas's lawyer. Have a good day," Trey said, waving me through to the front door. "Can I ask you something real quick?"

"Sure. What do you want to know?"

"What's Duncan Thomas like in real life?"

"Well, Trey, he's a real fucking prick."

"I thought so. All right, you have yourself a good day!"

6.

My previous interaction with Dr. Glacier had been brief, but the biggest takeaway was he was a big phony. After a decade of working for Duncan, I'd acquired the skill of spotting a fraud rather quickly. Dr. Glacier was just another middle school English teacher with a doctorate in poetry who fell ass-backward into becoming the head of school.

I had conducted some basic background intel on the Internet on the way over here. His parents were onetime hippies who'd sold out their rebellious spirit for a hefty corporate paycheck. This was a fairly typical path of most of the wealthy San Franciscans in the 1990s. Dr. Glacier had been raised like most coastal elite children of that time—politically correct, "enlightened" in civil rights, and greatly sympathetic for the poverty-stricken. Naturally, they grew up in exclusively white and affluent neighborhoods.

It was also clear from meeting him that he was a huge dweeb. He had certainly been bullied verbally and physically at some point in his life, creating trauma that likely remained with him to this very day. That meant my usual tough-guy routine and strong-arm approach would backfire. However, the issue of "bullying" could still be used to my advantage—as my stick *and* carrot against Larry.

Dr. Donovan Glacier tepidly opened the door and entered his office like a clumsy cat on roller skates and nearly tripped over himself before he awkwardly regained his balance.

"How are you, Mr. Cedar?" Dr. Glacier asked, avoiding eye contact.

Despite the fact that his personality and demeanor were opposite Duncan's, both men's confidence visibly grew upon sitting in their tall chairs behind their big desks, where they were "the man."

"Please call me Max," I replied. "You have a beautiful campus here, Dr. Glacier."

"Oh, thank you." He nodded in agreement. "And call me Donovan. Dr. Glacier is for the students."

"I appreciate that." I smiled.

If working for Duncan had taught me anything, it was how to butter up powerful men with fragile egos.

"So what can I do you for, Max?" Dr. Glacier asked.

"I don't know if you remember, but I was here about a year ago to see if my children could possibly enroll—"

"Of course! They live in New York with your wife. If I remember correctly, I believe you work here for Duncan Thomas."

"You have quite the memory, Dr. Glacier," I replied.

"Oh, yes, well, thank you. It would be tough to get a PhD with a bad memory." He laughed. "And please, call me Donovan."

"Well, Donovan, I think I may have finally convinced my wife to move out here with the children. She is very attached to her life in New York, but she acknowledges it's better to be together as a family."

"Yes, we all have to make sacrifices for family." Dr. Glacier solemnly nodded.

"I was hoping my son and daughter could attend a Jewish day school to maintain that aspect in their lives."

"I understand completely. That is why I am so happy that our school satisfies those special spiritual specifications, along with every single student's social and sensitive safety."

It sounded like he'd gone to the same poetry school as Dr. Seuss.

"That is so important to me, Dr. Glacier ... excuse me, Donovan. I wish all schools could be like that." I nodded, pretending like I knew what the hell he was talking about.

"Unfortunately, not all schools have the resources to do so."

"Yes, well, that was one of my concerns about this school actually."

Dr. Glacier nearly fell out of his expensive chair in shock. "Please, Max, share with me your concern."

"My dear friend's children currently attend the school and, without revealing the specifics, told me in confidence that his eldest son was in a situation pertaining to bullying—"

"Bullying? At this institution of education?" Dr. Glacier gasped. "Who is the parent? Your friend, what is his name?"

"Well, Dr. Glacier ..."

"Donovan."

"Donovan, as a lawyer, I am trained to keep personal discussions like these confidential. I'm sure you understand."

"Of course, I appreciate your caution. However, I must insist on knowing the name. Bullying is not only an emergency for the education system but a national emergency as well. It is simply intolerable."

"I could not agree with you more." I shook my head. "I'll give you his first name only—Larry."

"There is a parent named Larry who works for Mr. Duncan Thomas as well. Is it that Larry?"

"I cannot confirm whether or not it is him."

"Ah, I see, you cannot 'confirm' it," Dr. Glacier said with a wink.

"I just wanted to know where you stand on the issue of bullying. And, Donovan, I cannot express how happy I am with your concern on this important issue," I said as I stood up to leave.

"Oh, okay. Well, thank you, Max, so much for bringing this to my attention. And please let me know as soon as possible when you decide to enroll your children in our institution of education and sensitive spirituality," Dr. Glacier said, surprised the discussion had ended abruptly. I hoped he would ask about Larry's eldest son.

"Oh, before you go, Max, if I may inquire, can you tell me just one more detail? Is Oliver, excuse me, 'Larry's son', being bullied, or … is he the bully? Just between you and me, of course."

"Unfortunately, I can't reveal that. But I will get right back to you as soon as I discuss it with Larry."

"I certainly appreciate that, Max. Any information you could provide to us would be very beneficial."

I left the campus with a smile. I would make Larry's kid out to be the child from *The Omen* or that kid from *Jerry Maguire*—which one would depend on Larry.

7.

I understood why Larry did what he did. If I were in his situation, I would have done the exact same thing and betrayed him without hesitation. That was how it was for everyone in Duncan's orbit. It was "kill or be killed." I felt guilty about possibly destroying his child's future. But on the other hand, Larry had helped frame me for murder, extortion, and witness tampering, so he was not exactly a mensch.

Strategically, I called a few blocks away from Larry's house in case it was under surveillance by Duncan's goons and/or law enforcement. Since I was using a burner phone, I needed to convince him to answer an unknown number. Fortunately, Larry's appetite for knowledge was insatiable; he wanted to know everything about everybody. Betting on that hunger for knowledge to compel Larry to answer my call, I texted him: "Answer call for breaking news."

He answered on the second ring.

"Who the hell is this?" Larry demanded.

"It is your old friend from a long time ago," I responded.

"Max? I can't talk to you. You're a felonious thug—"

"Let's not get personal over the phone," I interrupted.

"I'm hanging up now."

"I only wanted to tell you I had a terrific meeting with Dr. Donovan Glacier today. I mentioned you."

"The headmaster of my kids' school? Mentioned me how? What the hell are you up to?"

"We just had a discussion about whether the school was a good fit for my children. I asked about his concern about bullying, and I mentioned how Oliver is involved in a nasty bullying incident currently."

"Oliver? My son? That is a load of bullshit!"

"Yeah, well, he wanted to know a lot more about it before he expelled anyone."

"Expel! What did you tell him, you motherless piece of shit?"

"Those were my thoughts exactly. I told him I would talk to you and get more information. I told him I would call him tomorrow to clarify the whole thing. He sounded quite eager to hear back from me."

Nearly a minute passed before Larry asked, "Where do you want to meet?"

"It's a nice day. We should go to the park and roam like the buffaloes."

"I will be there in one hour."

CHAPTER 6

Board Pieces

San Francisco, California

1.

The buffaloes were an allusion to the couple of dozen bison residing in Golden Gate Park. Duncan insisted on meeting his "people" at this spot. He loved watching the bison sit around and graze about and just doing nothing all day. At first, I believed the beasts amused him, but then I reconsidered that he was envious of them. Regardless, anyone who had worked for him knew it was his spot. Now, it was I watching the buffaloes roam while waiting to speak with Larry.

Despite the sky being covered in fog, it felt nice outside—low sixties with minor humidity and a timid breeze. It was necessary to be in control of this conversation from beginning to end. The options without Larry's cooperation were too dire to contemplate. As I spotted Larry approaching from a distance, it was clear he had to submit to my will.

Golden Gate Park was an ideal meeting location for guys like us. There were so many twists and turns, with hidden street signs that, even with GPS, you were guaranteed to get lost. However, Larry and I had come here many times; we could walk to this spot blindfolded.

"What the fuck, Max?" Larry asked.

"I should be asking you that, you two-timing son of a bitch!" I chirped back.

"Hey, I just gave you some money from Duncan. Anything else is between you and him."

"Give the innocent idiot act a rest. I know you were the point man for kidnapping London. Not to mention, you paid her off to frame me for Sarah Verand's murder!"

"How do you know …?" Larry stammered before regaining his composure. "That's all a bunch of bullshit. You were behind all of that Sarah stuff."

"Keep singing that same tune, Larry. It's not helping your kids' education any."

"What the fuck did you do, Max?"

"I told that *shmendrick* Dr. Glacier about your son's bullying situation."

"Is that it? Jesus, Max, that is some seriously weak leverage." Larry shook his head.

"I also paid an opportunistic fourth grader a hundred bucks to sing whatever song corroborates my story."

"What story?"

"That your dear boy Oliver is either an innocent victim of being bullied or … that he is physically, maybe even sexually, bullying this poor kid."

"Are you fucking serious, Max? You would do that to an innocent kid? That would destroy his life and our whole family!"

"In a New York minute. I've done worse than that. So have you, Larry, if you need reminding."

"What do you want?"

"I need your help, and confidence, from here on in. Your loyalty is to me now, not Duncan."

"What do I have to do for this wonderful opportunity?"

"I'll tell you soon enough. Right now, I only need your loyalty."

"Or what?"

"Your son is expelled, with a record of being a bully or, worse, a sex offender. Good luck getting into an Ivy League with that on your record."

"Just hearsay. All you have is some nitwit fourth grader in your corner."

"He is an effeminate, articulate little kid who is a star in his drama class."

"The little shit is in drama?"

"He's playing Peter Pan at the school production."

"Goddamn it! Okay, if I help you, what will the kid say?"

"That your son has protected him from another bully in school. I already have the perfect patsy in place. I scouted the school and found some fat, immature, awkward eighth grader. I bet I can work Dr. Glacier to be so appreciative he'll give you a discount on tuition for your son's heroics."

"How much off?"

"I bet I could cut a quarter off easily."

"For each of my kids?"

"I don't know about three kids."

"Twenty-five percent for each kid, for every year until graduation, for all of them. This fourth grader—dependable?"

"This kid is a star. Do you know how much a hundred dollars is for a ten-year-old? He'll come through, guaranteed."

Larry looked to the sky like he was receiving guidance from up above. With a deep sigh, he nodded in agreement. He departed quickly in the direction he'd come from. I stayed behind and observed the bison sleeping and chewing grass. I began to see the appeal. It must be wonderful to roam like a buffalo.

2.

By capturing Larry, I had taken a vital piece off Duncan's board. Even more, Larry was now my knight, who I could instruct to capture Duncan. To get to the king, I first had to get rid of the other main pieces of defense that were at Duncan's disposal. I'd only captured one of his critical pieces. Still on the board was his bishop, Richard, along with his newly anointed (and paid for) knight of his own when he'd turned London against me.

Duncan would do anything to protect his empire and, by extension, himself. My point of attack was based on convincing him that Junior was a pawn who must be sacrificed to avoid defeat. In the event Duncan was left unconvinced, plan B would be to turn Junior against Duncan. This would be a nearly impossible task. All Duncan's eldest ever wanted in his privileged life was Daddy's approval. Unfortunately for him, that was something that Duncan was incapable of giving, even and especially to his own son. I became red in embarrassment, realizing I desired the same fatherly approval from Duncan.

Junior's constant devotion to his father was why my head had nearly imploded in shock when London had confessed Junior was the culprit leaking her affair with Duncan to Sarah Verand. Were London and Junior so in love that her affair with his father had triggered Junior to do the impossible and betray his father? It seemed far-fetched, but so was the idea that Duncan would order the murder of a reporter. It would be naive of me to dismiss anything at this point. If Junior had betrayed Duncan once, he certainly would be willing to do so again. However, now squarely under Duncan's thumb, Junior would be under immense pressure to say so, as every effort would be made to ensure that Junior's first betrayal of his father would be his last.

That meant I needed more than a mere pawn to counterattack the offensive campaign being waged against me. I needed someone close to Duncan willing to turn on him if the price was right or the consequences were too severe to withstand. Most importantly, the individual needed to be devoid of a moral code. Fortuitously, Duncan exclusively kept company with people of that exact disposition. But it couldn't be any regular *putz* who worked for him. It had to be someone intelligent, with a grudge against Duncan and without an honest bone in his body. Before I finished my thought, I knew exactly who.

3.

The anecdote that best encompassed Joel Lewinsky occurred in the late '90s. A typical American might have been embarrassed to share a last name with the most famous female intern of all time for performing fellatio in the Oval Office. A right-wing nut, Joel was proud to be associated with the person at the center of bringing down the Democrat who was president of the United States of America at the time. Often he proclaimed, loudly enough for the various female secretaries to hear, "If I knew all we needed was a Lewinsky to blow the president to get him impeached, I would have offered up my services six years ago."

Joel easily checked off all the "shady and slimy" personality disposition boxes I needed to work with. It helped that he was an asshole for whom I had utter disregard. I had found that, the easier it was to convince myself that my targets had what was coming to them, the easier it was for me to push down the guilt of my actions. In fact, with Joel, it would be a real pleasure to bully him into (my) submission. If anyone had it coming in Duncan's inner circle, it was that pencil dick.

Every building built, hotel license acquired, and land deal approved in Duncan's empire always had a hidden amount that he would skim from. The obvious reason was to avoid paying taxes on the small fortune, but Duncan simply enjoyed earning money illegally. It had come to the point that, if Duncan could not figure out how to get "a cherry on top" (his description), he wouldn't even consider the deal. Eventually, Duncan's partners caught on and would add an insignificant "perk" (money) to every deal with Duncan and literally feign being upset at being "cheated" so Duncan would be amenable to the terms. What I knew that Duncan did not was that Joel skimmed off every illegally collected cent on every deal. If Duncan caught wind of this, it would be devastating to Joel's career and freedom, but the arrogant prick stole regardless. He never considered he might get caught, so he did not give one thought to the potential consequences.

Looking back on it, I was fortunate to have heard the end of a Duncan screaming rant directed at Joel a little while back. Having been on the receiving end of those rants dozens of times myself, I knew all too well the resentment and anger that was induced after such a verbal lashing from Duncan. Joel's fresh wound to his pride was a vulnerability that I would seize upon. I had to put the squeeze on him now, or else the beneficial storm of events would pass—and my opportunity along with it.

However, that was a task easier said than done. No doubt I was enemy number one to anybody who was directly associated with Duncan. Unlike Larry, Joel was such a sniveling sycophant of Duncan that he surely would be on the horn blabbing every detail to him the second I left him. I couldn't apply the pressure myself—it had to come from an outside source.

But who could effectively do that who had enough gravitas and stature that Joel wouldn't try, in some manner, to retaliate? While I tried to figure out what I should do, I stopped and witnessed two uniformed cops rudely telling a homeless person to piss off, or they would arrest him.

Suddenly I knew my next move, even if I dreaded just contemplating it.

4.

Despite swearing off all drugs and alcohol mere days earlier, I made an emergency exception and ate four marijuana cookies right before entering the San Francisco Police Department to turn myself in on my own recognizance. For my plan to work, I needed law enforcement on my side, which simply would be impossible as a fugitive. It was time to face the consequences and then try to avoid them to the best of my ability.

Barely two steps in from the front door, I saw Officer Smudge and Officer Crews. They spotted me so quickly that barely two seconds passed before both officers violently threw me to the ground and cuffed me.

"What the hell are you doing?" I asked with my face on the floor.

"You are a federal fugitive, and we are arresting you and handing you over to the FBI!" Officer Smudge sternly replied.

"I'm turning myself in!" I yelled back as Officer Crews lifted me to my feet.

"You can talk to the feds about all the details." Officer Smudge smirked, picking me up and throwing me toward the processing center.

"I need to talk to the chief," I protested.

"Chief is not in right now, tough guy. Anyway, it's not his jurisdiction, so it's not his case. The murder—"

"Alleged murder," I interrupted.

"The murder," Officer Smudge continued, "occurred in New Jersey. So you will be dealing with them, along with the FBI."

"But I need to tell the chief something important."

"Are you deaf? This doesn't concern the SFPD."

"But I have information about crimes that occurred in San Francisco!"

Officer Crews threw me down into a seat in the hall. I knew the drill from here. I would be fingerprinted, and then I would be in a holding cell with a bunch of drunk Neanderthals and local gang soldiers and drug dealers. For all the criminal acts I'd committed on Duncan's behalf, this was actually the first time I had been arrested. My chest began contracting, causing me to breathe rapidly with great difficulty. I was shvitzing like a desert dog in heat.

"Please," I begged with my head down in a daze. "It's about Duncan and his hotels." I could no longer keep my eyes open. I was losing consciousness. I was no longer in control. This time, I was sure I was having a stroke.

"Put him in my office," Chief Willard Williams said from down the hall. "I want to hear what he has to say."

5.

"What does any of this have to do with the murder of Sarah Verand?" Chief Willard Williams demanded impatiently.

"Joel is his right-hand man. He knows all the secrets. I am sure he knows what really happened with Sarah," I explained.

"I thought you were his right-hand man?" Chief Williamson asked.

"I am … or I was. As Duncan's legal representative, I had to maintain a 'legally clear conscience,' if you get what I'm saying." I winked.

"I don't know what the hell you're talking about." The chief threw up his hands in exasperation. "You are the main suspect in a murder, and you are blabbing like a teenager about dirty deals your client is brokering 'without your knowledge' but in the same breath telling me you are, in fact, aware of all illegal activities. Do you even have any evidence of this criminal behavior?"

"As I stated before, as Mr. Thomas's legal representative, I have no official knowledge of any illegal activity," I clarified.

"If you do not know anything, what good are you?"

"Because Joel knows all about it," I reiterated.

"About Sarah Verand's murder?"

"About the dirty deals. I strongly suspect he knows about Duncan's involvement in Sarah Verand's murder as well."

"This sounds like bullshit. The FBI agents will come to pick you up shortly."

"FBI? High-rises are being built on illegal backdoor deals with huge sums of money being stolen directly from the San Francisco taxpayer. Renters are getting squeezed tens of thousands of dollars a year because of their greed and profiteering. And you're just going to look the other way?"

"Isn't that exactly what you have done since working for Duncan?"

"I'm doing something about it now, aren't I?"

"A dollar short and a day late. This is about the murder of an innocent young woman, not about your path to redemption," the chief shot back and slowly exited the room.

"I will wear a wire." I sighed.

The chief slowly turned around. "Finally we can have a real discussion."

My body was trembling in shock after exiting the downtown police station. It was not pleasant, but the important thing was I'd left the station a free man, albeit under the supervision and responsibility of the FBI and SFPD. I'd never thought I would be a rat. I could not count the number of times I'd wrecked some poor shmuck trying to get out from under Duncan's grip doing the exact same thing. Duncan left me no other choice than becoming a state witness against him. Did he expect me to go to jail for something I did not do to protect him? It was brutally clear that he's never cared for me. I had simply been a pawn on *his* chessboard, moving at the whim of his "unmatched wisdom." The funny thing is, as deplorable as I previously found snitching to be, I felt okay about snitching on Duncan and downright giddy turning the screws on Joel.

The game between Duncan and me had officially begun, and we both had everything on the line to lose. His position was much stronger than mine. He had wealth, influence, power, and status as weapons against me. However, as David had his slingshot against Goliath, I had buried secrets to knock out Duncan. Duncan, like Goliath, underestimated my abilities. I, like David, had only one shot to take this behemoth out.

PART III

The Fix

CHAPTER 7

Pickles and Doughnuts

San Jose, California

1.

Finally, I was on my way to meet Duncan Thomas Jr. Duncan's inner circle referred to him as DTJ or Junior. At least those were the names he knew about. His actual nicknames were the Moron or the Little Bastard. For example, "Someone let the Moron know," or, "What did the Little Bastard do this time?" were frequent expressions on occasion when Duncan asked us to fix Junior's messes. We called him the Moron because the guy was dumb as nails. He posted monumentally preposterous things on social media, 90 percent of which were also incredibly offensive and usually bigoted. He got the name the Little Bastard because Duncan basically ignored his existence. The only time Duncan gave him any attention was when he did something that embarrassed him, which might explain why Junior was always screwing up. But likely it was because he was just an ignoramus.

Junior was always seeking his father's approval, which he never received, which caused him to lash out at everyone he could. He acted like a prince of Denmark when in the company of his father's employees, only to transform into a driveling little shit when his father entered the room. Everyone hated the Little Bastard, but as long as he had Duncan's name, we tolerated him and were forced to serve him. I had been assigned to protect and serve Duncan's "little bastard" many times. Of all the detestable things Duncan had commanded of me in the past, dealing with the Moron was by far the hardest to deal with.

Larry came through and helped me get a meeting with the Little Bastard. In return, I held up my end of the bargain by convincing Dr. Glacier that Larry's son was defending his fourth grade "pal" from being verbally abused and physically threatened by a school bully. Some thirteen-year-old fat loner named Dylan got kicked out of school when the young drama star I paid off corroborated the story. Dr. Glacier was so apologetic he gave all of Larry's children 25 percent off tuition (per my 'legal advice'). Though Larry did not like being squeezed, he was thrilled with the results.

The pretense given to Duncan Jr. for the meeting was unbeknownst to me. Larry just told me to go to the only kosher deli in San Jose, named Matt's. He promised me Junior would show, though I couldn't be completely confident; Larry might be setting me up. I might have been waiting for one of Duncan's thugs and would end up like Sarah Verand. At this point, it was a risk that had to be taken.

I sat down at a two-person booth in the back of the deli. I ordered a pastrami sandwich on rye and a cup of a matzo soup with a black cherry soda. If this was my last meal, it sure as hell wasn't going to be just water and free pickles. A half hour later, I had my last bite of pastrami and still no sign of him. Holy hell, the Little Bastard was a no-show. That prick Larry had played me!

I was about to leave to kick Larry's ass when I received a text message: "Hold tight. The Moron is coming now."

2.

It was hard to pinpoint precisely why everyone hated Junior. Numerous qualities rendered him detestable, but it was also the subtleness of those qualities. The first time I met him, he came across as a spoiled schmuck, but all in all, he seemed okay. Considering Duncan was his father, his daddy issues were unavoidable. Junior's childhood was what Luke Skywalker would have had if Darth Vader had raised him.

The expectations, which turned into responsibilities that he internalized, were considerable. Unfortunately for him, and his father, he was a dimwit. The millions of dollars spent on private education was a waste of money. Junior knew he was a moron, but more importantly, everyone else knew it. Above all else, his father knew it. The Little Bastard was always compensating. At first, he gave off this "earthly" charm, but eventually, his entitlement and fake "every guy" attitude became grating. His comments were inappropriate, bigoted, and always with a note of cruelty. In that way, he was very much like his father.

He entered the deli wearing a bright red designer-brand scarf and expensive winter jacket. The sight of him flooded my mind with all those irritating qualities I despised in him. But I needed Junior on my side, so I readied myself mentally to tolerate the Moron. First things first, I needed to make sure Junior would not bolt when he saw me. I casually turned my back to him as he searched the restaurant for whomever he thought he was meeting. I moved forward and to the left, necessitating physical contact between us when he passed me. The second I felt his shoulder rub against mine, I grabbed him by the shoulders and twisted him forward and threw him sternly in the empty seat in one motion. The table rattled and caused a bit of a stir. I patted Junior on the back like we were good friends from high school. He tried to get up and flee once he saw my face. I jumped up and gave him a huge hug and held him extremely tight. With a huge grin, I whispered in Junior's ear, "Sit your ass down, or I take you out back."

"Have a seat!" I yelled enthusiastically to show the other patrons this was a happy reunion between friends.

Junior stared back at me, visibly contemplating fleeing again.

"It has been so long!" I continued loudly. "I just came back from speaking with your father."

"You spoke to Dad?" Junior asked quizzically.

"Yeah, about his business in London," I responded with the same wide smile.

"L-L-London?" Junior stammered.

"I thought you knew about your dad and his business *in* London? Sit down. We can talk about it."

Junior nervously checked around the restaurant to see if anyone was watching him. He was fidgeting so profusely it looked like he had to take a shit in the middle of the delicatessen.

"Relax, okay? I am just here to talk to you, all right?"

"Fuck you, Max," Junior whispered loudly.

"It might not seem like it, but I am here to help you."

"Help me? Bullshit. You are here to save your ass."

"True, but helping you helps save my ass."

"Help me help you? You're not Jerry McGuire, Max."

"Call me whatever you want, but I am the guy who will get you what you want."

"And what is it that I want exactly?"

"To get you out from under your father's thumb."

"Why would I want that? I have everything. I am truly blessed to be the son of Duncan Thomas."

"Is that so?"

"Beautiful women, private planes, great job, and family. What could you possibly offer me that would be better than that?"

"Something your father never gave you," I said to Junior.

I ate the front half of the biggest pickle on the table while maintaining aggressive eye contact.

Junior's face conveyed not only skepticism but also curiosity about what I was going to say. "Well, what the fuck is it?"

"Respect," I calmly responded as I chopped down the second half of the pickle.

"My father respects me," Junior scoffed.

"The hell he does. He thinks you are a bona fide loser."

"That's bullshit."

"You know what your nickname is with the guys?"

"I don't want to know. Besides, you're full of shit."

"It's Little Bastard because of how much your dad hates you."

"That is just because all of you guys are jealous of me."

"Your father thinks you're a dumbass."

"How would you know that?"

"Because he's always saying, 'I don't know what happened, but the kid is a dumbass.'"

"He said that about me?"

"He has no respect for you at all."

"But I have his name."

"The name is the main reason for his contempt. He even told me once he almost renamed you to—"

"Todd?" he interrupted.

"How did you know that?"

"In high school, he called me Todd for a year. I never knew why. I thought it was a joke or some cool nickname. I guess he was just trying it out to see if it stuck."

"See, your father hates you. He slept with London purely to disrespect you."

"He slept with London?"

"You didn't know? That is what this whole mess is about in the first place."

"He said it was because of my affair with London. He blames me for the whole reporter business because I was going to bring down the family name. That's why he's putting me up in the hotel until this all blows over."

"He isn't putting you up. He's imprisoning you in that hotel room so you don't expose his affair."

"I hate him!" Junior slammed his right fist on the table, causing all the other patrons of the deli to look over to check out the commotion. "I am going to kill him!"

"No need." I put my hands up to calm him down. "All you have to do is cooperate with my plan. He will get his comeuppance. Believe me on that."

"Plan? What are you up to, Max?" Junior asked.

"I'll tell you all you need to know when the time comes. But for now, just get in touch with me through Larry."

"Larry knew about this too? That piece of garbage!"

"We need Larry, okay? He is integral."

"I don't know, Max. My father always gets what he wants in the end. You should know that better than anyone."

"That's why I am the guy to fix everything. I know Duncan's tricks. This is exactly the kind of stuff I get paid to do."

Junior got up to leave, shaking his head. "I just hope he didn't hurt the baby," he said.

"What baby?" I asked.

"London didn't tell you? She's pregnant with my kid. How did you not know that?"

"London is pregnant?"

"Yes, of course. Our love child is why my dad was so angry with me. I guess you don't know everything, Max."

Junior left the deli in a hurry as I ate the last pickle on the plate. Junior was a moron, but he was right: I didn't know shit.

3.

No wonder Duncan was going to such great (and criminal) lengths to cover up this *verkakte* situation. He was having a love child with a stripper, which would ruin his image; his marriage; his family; and, most importantly to him, his business. Or he had an affair with a stripper while she was pregnant with his grandson, which would have an even worse fallout. However, it was still hard to believe he would authorize the murder of a reporter. There was still something I was missing—a wrinkled corner that I needed to smooth over. I didn't have time to figure that aspect out right now. The train was already on the rails, and I needed to make sure it went on the right tracks.

Joel Lewinsky was a crucial cog in the plan, but his participation was far from a guarantee. Putting the squeeze on him would take some tactical maneuvering. The guy was a weasel—if I approached him about working this with me, his instinct would be to immediately squeal the entire plan to Duncan. I had to entice him with a carrot or beat him with a very large stick. If that didn't work, I always had an ace up my sleeve. It was a dirty play that I would be ordinarily reluctant to utilize, but for Joel, it would be a pleasure to make an exception.

The feds sending Joel to a maximum-security prison was my big stick. What would an enticing carrot be? Conducting a quick psychological profile of Joel, I concluded he was a brash, arrogant, and narcissistic white male with deeply rooted insecurities. A pang reverberated in my chest; those characteristics applied to nearly all of Duncan's employees, myself included. Duncan molded his soldiers (servants) in his image. Even having personally gone through it, I was not sure how he controlled people's behavior to such an impactful magnitude.

I took some relief in the fact that Joel was quantifiably a bigger asshole than me. He had absolutely no shame, as demonstrated by his ignoramus behavior. He was quite possibly the most annoying individual I had ever come across. His eagerness to please Duncan was sickening; he acted like the brownnosing student who brought his teacher an apple in the morning and a hand job after school.

The only person who even came close to being that pathetic in trying to please Duncan was his son, Junior. In a way, Duncan's collection of "employees" (thugs) all had an issue with trying to please their fathers. Duncan saw this trait in all of us and then used it to manipulate us to do his bidding. We all craved the approval and discipline only a father could provide, and he fittingly manipulated us with praise and abused us with humiliation. He pitted us up against one another, which in turn made everyone else who worked for Duncan a mortal enemy. I needed to outduel Joel to survive.

4.

Being outside the purview of Duncan was the primary factor in San Jose being my choice of place to meet Joel. It was a big city with a diverse population that aptly facilitated a low profile. With Silicon Valley located in San Jose, it also provided a credible pretense for Joel to schlep all the way over to the South Bay. Larry told Joel that Duncan was getting into the tech business and needed Joel to meet the potential partner down in the valley. Larry even gave Joel a fake CEO name of a fake business—Harry Fuchs of the tech giant LITTER. Joel was practically halfway down the 280 South freeway the instant Larry mentioned there could be some percentage points in it for him if he could close the deal.

I was waiting in the popular South Bay doughnut chain Crazy Donuts! The doughnuts here had strange combinations that appeared disgusting, yet every bite was a mini-orgasm in your mouth. I had anxiously eaten nearly a dozen different combinations anticipating Joel's arrival. I had just finished a Bacon Squeal Meal Donut (bacon bits on maple icing and chocolate chips) when I began to feel gassy. I began to burp, and the belches were growing louder and louder. Soon after, I farted uncontrollably and consistently. Gradually, the assault to the sense of smell was unbearable for everyone in the shop. Ten minutes into my human methane monstrosity, everyone within earshot (and smelling distance) from me had left. Barely eaten doughnuts were left on nearly all the tables from the rush to exit the shop.

I took advantage of the rash of empty seats and tactically sat so Joel would not be able to see me when he entered the shop, yet I could see him in the reflection from the glass wall. His irritating, shit-eating grin was easy to spot a mile away. He was clearly looking around for "Harry Fuchs, the CEO of LITTER" immediately after he strutted through the entrance door. As I was the only person in the joint, he walked toward me.

His shit-eating grin slowly transformed into a crunched-up face of disgust when the stench of my bowel gasses attacked his nostrils. Joel was visibly gagging as he tapped me on the shoulder and asked, "Are you Harry Fuchs, CEO of LITTER?" I turned around and shoved Joel into my booth against the wall, similar to my action against Junior at the delicatessen. Before he knew what was happening, I sat so close to him his left cheek was against the glass wall and his right cheek against my sweaty shirt. Between the heat, the stench, and near drowning in the perspiration of my armpit, Joel desperately tried to get around me to leave. However, his body weight of 140 pounds stood no chance against me. He was slowly being crushed against the window, and every desperate breath of air came with the vile stench of my farts and belches, which I continued to produce.

"What the fuck, Max?" Joel gasped.

"I am going to move. When I do, you are just going to sit there all nice and quiet, or you'll end up back here in this exact position. You get me?"

"Just get the fuck off me already!" Joel, nearly in tears, yelled.

"Nice and quiet, got it?"

"For fuck's sake, I got it. Just get the hell off me!"

Slowly relaxing the pressure, I moved about a half foot away in the other direction. He quickly shot up and instinctively stretched, gasping for air.

"Oh my god, I can taste your farts!" Joel coughed.

"I swear that was not part of the plan." I smiled.

"Get the hell out of my way! I can't take another second smelling whatever the fuck is oozing out of you! Besides, you are a criminal, and Duncan wants your head on his wall."

"That is why I need your help."

"You got to be shitting me right now, literally and figuratively. Besides, even if I liked you, I wouldn't help you, and I don't fucking like you!"

"I am not so fond of you myself, Joel."

"Then what the fuck am I doing here smelling your stinky asshole?"

"As I said, I need your help, and you are going to oblige me."

"The hell I am!"

"I could tell Duncan about how you are skimming off the top on every single deal and transaction you have ever made with him," I replied.

"That's a bunch of bullshit. I have never taken a dime more than I am owed!"

I had to give the guy some credit. His denials were always forceful and with conviction. If I didn't know better, I might have believed him.

Unfortunately for him, I did. "I am not going to argue about facts. Larry has the proof."

"Damn it, that son of a—"

"Don't worry, I don't care about what you stole. I just need your help. It might even be to your advantage. Of course, that depends if you can keep your mouth shut."

"I don't care whatever drug deal you and Larry cooked up together. You are creating false evidence to justify your libelous allegations against me. I will gladly smell your disgusting gas toxins all day before I help you bring down my mentor, Duncan, who I love—"

"You help me, you keep all the money you stole; no questions asked," I interrupted his dramatic spiel.

Joel paused to consider my offer before continuing, "A man who I love and admire. Furthermore, to deride my character and, more importantly, my reputation is unacceptable—"

"You will be able to screw Junior out of his job and maybe replace him as CFO."

"Okay, I'm in," Joel responded instantly. "Now please, I need to leave immediately. I can't breathe back here!"

CHAPTER 8

Closing Time

San Francisco, California

1.

The stink of Joel's character (and my flatulence) stuck to me the entire drive up to San Francisco. Since the very beginning of my tenure under Duncan, I'd justified dealing with sleazebags, and occasionally being one myself, by having a cynical outlook—to "succeed" I needed to be a ruthless asshole without any remorse. Currently, I was a ruthless asshole just to keep my *tuchus* out of jail. It helped that I was screwing over a group of people who deserved their comeuppance. Besides, after working for Duncan all these years I was well versed in burying any guilt that could afflict me.

I collapsed on the bed instantly upon entering my motel room. I was too tired to function and too anxious to sleep. There were a lot of balls in the air, but at least I hadn't dropped any juggling them—yet. Intellectually, I was always aware that I would face Duncan sooner or later. However, the reality of it was hitting me for the first time. I had never seriously confronted him. I was not sure of my ability (and vulnerability) when it came to a face-to-face battle. My entire plan and future depended on me successfully destroying Duncan. At a minimum, I had my doubts about a positive outcome.

Joel, as loathsome as he was, was a gold mine of information. Leverage is knowledge. At last, I had an upper hand on all the parties I was dealing with—more than the feds, more than Junior or London, and now even more than Duncan. Being Duncan's fixer had taught me that the key to leverage was applying it to your benefit in every possible way. At times, that meant mixing fact and fiction. Once the mark could not tell the difference, he or she became a sucker. Once a sucker, the screws could be turned against the target, followed by an offer that could not be refused. Less than a week ago, I was convinced that what benefited Duncan benefited me as well. In reality, I had been the sucker the whole time.

Before I approached Duncan, there was one more matter that I had to successfully complete. It would take a lot of pressure and persuasive bullshit to pull off. Luckily, those were the two prominent characteristics of my profession. Though I was reluctant to speak to London due to her personal betrayal, she was vital to the fix. There was no love lost between us, but a genuine connection had been made in Las Vegas, and that would go a long way in turning her against Duncan. Duncan, however, was not the only target I needed her to betray.

2.

London's apartment was assuredly under surveillance by the police and/ or Duncan's henchmen. Officially, I had an agreement to turn witness with the feds via the SFPD, but I could not be sure that all the lawmen involved were in the know. Furthermore, I could not trust that Chief Willard Williams wouldn't hang me out to dry if the action against Duncan went south. Fortuitously, London's building was the first of four apartment buildings connected through several entrances on different floors. I entered the residence building opposite London's, labeled D building, which was a half mile from the A building where London's apartment was located.

The apartments were on a typical San Francisco hilly area, so the floors from building to building did not match up. The A and B buildings had the garage as the first floor, whereas the first floor for the C and D buildings was the lobby. Meanwhile, the B and C buildings had a backyard area filled with oak trees, while the D building had direct access to the community pool and management offices. After walking for almost an hour in the maze, I was officially lost. Initially, I thought I was entering the C building, only to end up in the pool area. After backtracking, I got lost in the garage crossing from the C to B buildings. Twenty minutes later, I nearly walked off the roof trying to find where building B and A connected. Eventually, I found the correct entrance and arrived at London's building, successfully avoiding detection.

I sternly knocked on the door. I had to convince London to turn on Duncan despite being in his (pants) pocket. I was the absolute wrong messenger to argue the virtue of morality, so I would have to authentically connect with her for her to help me. Whether it was a stripper like London or a crooked lawyer like myself, people hated being treated like trash after no longer having any "value." Regrettably, from undergoing the same trauma, I knew how it felt.

To my surprise, London opened the door after only a few knocks.

"What are you doing here, Max?"

"London, nice to see you. May I come in?"

"I have nothing to say to you!" London replied before trying to slam the door in my face.

I stopped the door from closing with the end of my leather shoes.

"You don't need to say anything. Just listen, please," I pleaded.

"Everything you say is a lie!"

"London, I know we have a strained relationship. I have done some things to you—"

"Damn right!" London yelled, attempting to close the door again.

This time, I held the door open with my shoulder. "And you have done some things to me."

"Are you doing the 'poor-me' thing again, Max?"

"No, I am doing the let's-fuck-over-Duncan thing, and all I need you to do is listen."

"Talk!"

"Well, first you have to let me in," I stammered. "Then all you have to do is listen."

With a heavy sigh and a light shrug, London pulled the door open for me to come in.

After withstanding the multiple physical and verbal assaults from London she'd dealt me once she'd closed the door, I finally offered my proposition.

"Do you really think you can pull this off?" she asked.

"My determination is strong. I won't let any emotion stop me from resolving this. If that means taking down my former mentor—hell, even father figure—then that is what I will do. It won't be easy, but when it comes down to it, you can count on me."

"No," she replied, shaking her head. "I mean, do you think *you* can pull this off? Like, are you competent enough to do it? Or smart enough?"

"You don't think I'm smart enough?" I asked with a half grin.

London stared back at me without answering.

"Well, don't you?"

"I'm thinking," London replied. "Maybe."

3.

Admittedly, I was proud, as well as shocked, at how well things had turned out so far. All the dominoes were set. All I needed was the "Goldilocks" of pushes—not too strong but not too soft. Luckily, I had a decade of experience exerting the precise amount of velocity necessary. That did not mean I wasn't nervous as hell. My stroke symptoms occurred hourly. But I remained focused and, more importantly, sober.

The remaining obstacle ahead was somehow convincing Duncan to meet me in person, preferably alone. This would be a difficult task under ordinary circumstances, and these circumstances were anything but ordinary. A weakness of Duncan to attack was the thing Duncan hated most in the world—bad press. I knew exactly who to contact: Sarah Verand's editor, Chase Toad, the man on television talking about her days earlier. Certainly, the possibility that he would alert the authorities upon my contacting him existed. Thankfully, I was already an informant. Moreover, a journalist like Chase would go to nearly any lengths to get the scoop. In that sense, journalists were like dogs, and I had an exceptional bone to throw his way.

I rummaged online to find a contact number for Chase. I'd had several interactions with him before, none of which has been pleasant for either one of us. Chase, more than anything, was a dork. He was plenty smart, yet he behaved like an idiot. He liked being a "big shot," but in reality, no one respected him. Every interview Chase conducted he constantly interrupted the other person with an irrelevant fact. Also, he hammered home a point unnecessarily. He took himself very seriously even though he worked at a second-rate print paper. His labored attempts at jokes were never funny and always awkward. Frankly, he never shut up yet never had anything interesting to say.

After four rings, a woman answered, asking how she could assist me.

"I would like to speak with Chase Toad," I said.

"Who may I ask is calling?" the woman asked.

"Tell him it is a friend of Sarah's," I replied.

"What is your name?" she asked.

"I just told you. I am a friend of Sarah's," I replied.

"But what is your name, sir?" she asked again.

"Listen, please tell Chase I have information regarding the suspicious death of Sarah Verand."

"Sure thing. And your name, sir?"

"I am not going to tell you my name, got it, sister? Put Chase on the line, or I go to the *Post* with this information."

"Okay, just a moment. I am connecting you with Chase right now," she replied.

As I waited for Chase to pick up the phone, I could clearly hear the lady speaking in the background.

"Hey, Chase, pick up the phone!" she yelled.

"Who is it?" Chase asked.

"I don't know! The pushy prick wouldn't say."

"What does he want?"

"Something about Sarah getting killed."

"What about it?"

"I don't know! Just pick up the damn phone before I smack you with it!"

"Fine." Chase came on the line. "Who is this?"

"Jesus, have you guys ever heard of an anonymous source before?"

"I don't play games when it comes to Sarah. You said you know something about her murder, so spill it!"

I had to admit, I was impressed with the authority and conviction in his tone. "Okay, Chase. It's Max."

"Max who?"

"Max Cedar, Duncan's private attorney." I sighed.

"You're Duncan's fixer?" Chase asked.

"His private attorney," I corrected him. "We've met before."

"I know exactly who you are. I should call the police!" Chase responded.

"Chase, I didn't kill Sarah, but I have a story for you."

"I should call the police!"

"Listen, Chase, I have the story Sarah was working on—the one that got her killed."

There was a considerable pause until Chase asked, "The one on Duncan?"

"Exactly. Duncan had an affair with a stripper named London—"

"Just so you know," Chase interrupted, "I should call the police, and we knew about the Duncan and London thing already."

"Did you know another person in Duncan's inner circle was also having an affair with London?" I asked.

"Okay, please continue. But I should call the police—"

"His very own son."

"Duncan Thomas Jr.?" Chase gasped. "And London will confirm the whole thing? An exclusive?"

"That is why I'm calling you first."

"You know I should call the—"

"Do you want the story or not?"

"Yes, absolutely, please, or thank you. You said exclusive, right?"

4.

I imagined Duncan's fat face turning red with rage as I watched Chase Toad's interview with London live on my cell phone. In addition to the editor of a paper, Chase was a contributor to the web news series *LIT* (*Live Interviews Today*), which was streaming the exclusive on social media platforms. It had surpassed one million views a mere two minutes into the broadcast, with guaranteed millions more to be added throughout the interview.

Chase had printed the story of the torrid affair between Duncan and London in the *New Jersey News* the night before, which had subsequently been picked up by every cable news channel and political website worth a damn. In the last sentence of his article, Chase had teased another bombshell: "In addition to the affair, our source indicated that London had an intimate relationship with someone in Trump's inner circle. To find out who, stay tuned!"

"Who is the other guy?" was the number one trending topic in the nation. Everyone in the country made a prediction of who it could be. The guesses were all over the place. Nearly 1 percent of several polls even voted me as the "other guy." Duncan surely abhorred the public humiliation. Chase Toad, who Duncan spitefully referred to as the "nerdy virgin," had exposed Duncan by parading his lover against him. I would be surprised if any furniture in Duncan's office had survived when the interview was over.

"Do you regret having an intimate relationship with Duncan Thomas?" Chase asked London after a short break.

"Do you mean having sex with him?" London said.

"Right, basically, sure, I mean, yes," Chase stammered.

"Yes, I do. It was very painful. Not just for me but for his wife and family also."

"Speaking of his family—"

"And the sex was awful. The only good thing was how quickly it took him to—"

"If we could pivot away from that topic. You mentioned his family—"

"And his penis was small, which in this case was actually a good thing."

The interview was doing far better than I had anticipated.

"Okay," Chase continued after a long pause, "circling back to Duncan's family. You mentioned you hurt them with this affair. Was there any family member, in particular, that was hurt by this?"

"His wife." London nodded.

"Besides his wife," Chase impatiently replied. "Another close relative, maybe?"

"Yes, there is, Chase," London said with tears in her eyes.

After waiting for London, Chase asked, "Who would that be?"

"Duncan's son."

"Can you be more specific?"

"Duncan Thomas Jr."

"Why him? Is it because you were having an affair not only with his father but also with him—and at the same time?"

Here came the bombshell to force Duncan's hand.

"Yes, I had an affair with DTJ before Duncan intervened and broke us up."

Not only had I screwed over Duncan, but I'd also managed to turn his son against him in one fell swoop.

"And we love each other!" London continued.

Sweat poured from my forehead. She shouldn't be saying this. Oh well, as long as she didn't mention the pregnancy …

"And I am carrying his baby!"

5.

London had just blown up my last piece of leverage. Duncan could now make arrangements with his son to get their story straight and agree who the father was. Duncan could live with the rumors—as long as he controlled the narrative. The interview was successful in creating a rift between father and son. Hopefully, it would be big enough for me to climb through and fix this.

Regardless, knowing Duncan as I did, I was certain the Chase Toad interview had him completely shaken. His instinct would be to hit back at whoever had caused this humiliation; I was directly in his scope now. In past circumstances, I would be terrified of the unbridled rage coming my way. Now I was depending on it.

The urge to smoke and drink my impatient anxiety away waiting for Duncan to call was tremendous. Still, I remained strong and resisted that temptation. After what felt like an eternity, my phone buzzed. It was Joel Lewinsky. I knew he was calling on behalf of Duncan. That piece of shit played both sides as well as anybody.

"You there, Max?" Joel asked.

After a deep pause, I replied, "What the hell are you doing, Joel?"

"Duncan wants to talk with you," he said.

"About what?"

"You are too ugly to be cute, Max."

"You fucking snake. Does Duncan know the part you played in all of this?"

"It was nice catching up with you, Max. Stop by for drinks tonight, eight sharp."

6.

Like so many times before, I pressed the top button to Duncan's office. Unlike before, this time, I felt like a stranger. Duncan had been everything to me—mentor, savior, and father. He may still be a king; he was no longer my ruler. Regardless of the outcome, I had attained my freedom. I entered Duncan's office like a gladiator ready to take on the mad emperor in his very own arena.

Duncan was seated in his oversized chair behind his tiny desk, flanked by Joel and Larry standing on each side. This was clearly orchestrated to intimidate me. Everything with Duncan was a show performed for maximum effect. He lived his life as if he were on a television show that was continuously filming without any cameras.

"Have a seat, Max," Joel sniveled.

"Hey, Larry, I had no idea you would be here also," I said with a phony smile.

He could barely nod in response before looking down to avoid any eye contact.

"You're not here to talk to Larry, Max," Joel remarked.

"So what the fuck am I doing here?" I replied.

"Sit down, Max. You are making a fool of yourself," Duncan finally interjected.

I took a seat at his command like a well-trained dog. The confidence I had mere seconds earlier had diminished just like that.

"Now, Max," Joel continued, "We called you in to discuss your behavior."

"My behavior? I am not the one trying to set up a loyal employee and a devoted friend for murder," I replied.

Duncan sighed deeply, visibly frustrated that I was defending myself.

"Max, you're a smart guy. A shitty lawyer, but a smart guy," Joel said.

"Joel, do me a favor. Shut the hell up already," I snipped.

"Listen here, we are calling the shots here—"

"We? I am here to speak with Duncan."

"Well, I am speaking on behalf of Duncan."

"I told you to shut the fuck up!" I yelled, stopping Joel in his tracks. "Duncan, you know this guy is playing you, right? He already gave me everything I need to take you down."

"What is he talking about?" Duncan turned to Joel.

"You can't believe a word he says! He is just trying to save his own ass!" Joel shouted.

"He also stole from you on every deal you ever made," I added.

"That is a bunch of bullshit! You can't believe a word this traitor says," Joel cried out. "I would never do that to you!"

"I can prove it," I said, handing Duncan the paper trail of Joel skimming from the top for years. Duncan was not the brightest bulb, but he knew how to read any document that had his money on it. The murderous gaze he gave Joel indicated he agreed with my accusation.

"You should also know that your Queen's Guard on your other side there, not saying a word, has been helping me this whole time." I pointed to Larry.

"What the fuck did you do, Larry?" Duncan growled.

In sharp contrast to Joel, Larry sheepishly shrugged his shoulders, staring at the ground. Duncan furiously shook his head, still flipping through the papers.

"Both of you, get out of my office," Duncan said quietly.

"Boss, come on, you don't believe him, do you?" Joel asked shakily.

"Get the fuck out!" Duncan yelled.

Joel put his head down in shame and exited with tears in his eyes. Larry followed Joel sheepishly without a sound.

After he straightened his suit jacket and took his seat, Duncan asked, "You ready to talk now?"

7.

The Penn and Teller performance by Joel and Larry had caught me off guard, but I'd managed to take them out of the equation. Though Duncan could be a great manipulator in one-on-one conversations, he also was easier to deal with without an audience to impress. This was especially true when it came to business. In front of others, he did his usual "I-am-a-great-negotiator" shtick and just refused every offer. Without anyone to witness the negotiation, it allowed him to frame the facts and boast about how he "totally won the negotiation." The individual on the other end of the deal went along with whatever Duncan said because, in reality, Duncan always got completely fleeced. Duncan did not care about actually getting a good deal; he just liked making deals and then bragging about them. Every business partner of his simply complimented him and enabled his belief that he got the better end of the deal. No longer under his spell, I saw with abundantly clarity that Duncan was the worst businessman I had ever met. His success did not lie in his acumen but, rather, in his ability to manipulate everyone to perceive him as he perceived himself—the best of the best and a gift to the universe.

"Max, I must tell you, I am very impressed with what you have done here." This was where Duncan was at his best. He flattered people to build them up, only to later chop them down. His compliments rekindled the warm feelings I'd received from his previous praise of me. In that instant, I'd been starved for more of his adoration.

"I am not here for the compliments." I snapped out of his seduction. "I came to do business."

"You call this business, Max?" Duncan asked.

"I learned it from you."

"You are nothing like me—never were, never will be. That's your last lesson, but that was the first thing you should have learned."

"You're right about that, Duncan. I wanted to be you. Now I'm damn relieved I never will be."

"Max, what can I say? You played your cards well, but it was a losing hand."

"So what now? I take the rap for this Sarah Verand murder?"

"No one murdered Sarah!" Duncan pounded the table. "I don't do that."

Duncan got up from his oversized chair and walked toward the window with a view of the entire city toward Oakland. The Bay Bridge was all lit up, making the picture outside of Duncan's tower particularly stunning. "It was a miscommunication. I only said it to get rid of her. I never said anything about killing anybody!"

8

Duncan frequently proclaimed he would have been an amazing general had he enlisted in the army. "If it was not for my broken index toe," he would proclaim, "I would have joined the army. And believe me, I would have been a general in a couple of years. There wouldn't have been anyone promoted to general faster than me."

Like a general, he gave orders. However, unlike a general, his orders were vague, so he could always maintain plausible deniability. This meant that to be in his personal employment required fluency in "Duncan speak." Like with any foreign language, some people interpreted "Duncan speak" differently. And many times, things got lost in translation. What was Duncan's actual intention? Only he knew for certain. Either way, he had given the code red, and as a direct consequence, Sarah was dead.

"This would never have happened if you did your job in the first place!" Duncan pointed his finger at me like he was Zeus with a lightning bolt.

Outraged, I resisted the urge to get visibly upset with Duncan placing the blame on me by demeaning my professional competence. I knew this was Duncan's opening tactic for negotiation. Despite the simplicity, it was effective. Nonetheless, I couldn't let his bullshit slide without defending myself. "You kept me in the dark the whole time. I was playing the hand blind. If you would have told me you cheated with London on your own son—"

"She came onto me!" Duncan shot back.

"You also didn't tell me about how London was pregnant with your kid."

"That bastard is not my kid. It's my grandkid, and that's all there is to it!"

I took a second before I responded. Duncan had showed his hand. He was going to officially state his potential love child with London was actually his grandchild. Too late to cover up the affair and child; he was going to spin it the best he could. London was paid to confirm it was Junior's, and a corrupt doctor would be paid to fabricate the DNA results.

"Okay." I nodded. "I have a plan."

"Who the fuck do you think you are, Max?"

"The fucking fixer. And we are dealing with one huge fucking mess."

9

"It looks like you really thought this one through." Duncan nodded.

"This was the only option that keeps me out of jail and prevents me from ending up like Sarah," I replied.

I had laid out my strategy for him. We agreed on the generalities, yet we both knew the details determined the winner and loser of the deal. I was wary of Duncan's disposition to throw in a last-second condition when he felt he was getting swindled.

"I don't like it. Junior is not tough like me. He'll be a flipper," Duncan said.

"He's been kept in the dark the whole time. He does not have anything to offer up against you—at least nothing that could be substantiated. Plus, with the evidence we have against him, it won't even matter."

"He is my son. But he is too stupid to shave money off the top of all my deals and launder it to offshore accounts by forging the paperwork to appear as business expenses and avoid taxes. This whole thing has to be over after all this. He won't be enough. We need someone else also."

"That is exactly why we are implicating Joel as his accomplice to the fraud. We prove that Junior and Joel have been running this scheme without your knowledge. It works, especially since Joel has been actually stealing from you. Besides, he betrayed you by helping me in the first place."

Duncan stroked his fat chin with his small hands. "Can we count on Joel?"

"He'll do a year or so in some fancy prison upstate. Promise him a job and some money when he gets released to keep his mouth shut. And if he is still a putz and does not agree, we simply turn over all the paper evidence Larry has saved against Joel. Plenty to charge him with from working for you."

"Fine. We pin the murder on Junior."

"I testify that Sarah was going to report on his affair and love child with London. You get your guy to testify too—that Junior ordered him. Will he agree to that?"

"Don't worry about him. He is a loyal soldier."

"So to be clear—Junior was stealing funds with Joel's help. After Junior found out about your affair with London, he wanted to set you up for the murder to take over the company."

Duncan continued to nod. "Just one more thing. You're out! I don't want to see your face in my building or this city or even state! You're done, Max!"

"Deal!" I extended my hand, which Duncan reluctantly shook.

Despite my certainty that I was going to die of heart complications at any moment, I exited the room with a smile.

CHAPTER 9

Loose Ends

New York, New York

1

Duncan Thomas Jr.'s arrest was reported by every newspaper, magazine, television channel, and website possible. San Francisco Police Chief Willard Williams was scheduled to officially announce the charges against him momentarily. Chase Toad had already broken the story the night before in the *New Jersey News*. Fittingly, the very paper Sarah Verand worked for broke the arrest of her killer. In fact, Sarah's name was in the byline as the coauthor of the piece. Unfortunately, she died in the process, but at least it got published in the end.

Immediately following Chief Willard Williams's press conference, Chase had an exclusive with *the* Duncan Thomas in the flesh. Though I felt disgusted that I helped Duncan literally get away with murder, I could not help but feel the pride of being the conductor of an orchestra of cover-up and propaganda. Most importantly, I felt relief that this mess was behind me.

My wife and the kids were attending a kid's birthday party somewhere in Brooklyn. I was not sure when they would be back, but we were having a Passover Seder dinner at my father's apartment in less than an hour. Zevi and I were sharing a Nova Scotia bagel from Barney's while watching the news. Despite my wife and I getting along well since I'd quit working for Duncan and returned home, after being back for three days, I already needed a break from the family life. The adjustment from slick, intimidating lawyer to normal civilian with a family was not simple.

Zevi barked when Chief Willard Williams appeared on the television screen. I appreciated the sentiment, but I told him to hush up. I wanted to hear what the guy was going to say.

"First, I would like to thank the many officers of law enforcement who helped solve this tragic murder of Sarah Verand, in particular the FBI, along with the cooperation of the New York and New Jersey police departments."

Everyone received adulation except for the individual who'd handed the chief, the feds, and Duncan the perfect solution on a silver fucking platter—me. Don't get me wrong; I was glad to be sitting on my couch in my living room instead of some stone bed in a cage. Nevertheless, seeing others take credit for your work, whether it was a megalomaniacal billionaire or the chief of police, was infuriating.

"At 6:04 this morning, a raid was conducted by the San Francisco Police Department, under the surveillance of the Federal Bureau Investigation, into an apartment located in the Presidio Heights belonging to Duncan Thomas II, also known as Duncan Thomas Jr., aka DTJ, or most commonly referred to as Junior and referenced by colorful nicknames by his associates."

"Get to the damn point already!" I yelled out loud, and Zevi barked at the television.

"A preponderance of evidence was discovered and then collected and finally reported of the direct involvement in the murder of Sarah Verand," the chief finally announced.

Though I expected this outcome, I nearly choked on my bagel officially hearing Junior was going down for his father's crime.

"A short time ago, Duncan Thomas Jr. confessed to contracting a murder-for-hire scheme. At this time, the killer who was hired to kill Ms. Verand is being pursued in an undisclosed location somewhere in the tri-state area. Additionally, Duncan Thomas Jr. confessed his crime to his mistress and mother to his unborn son, London Brood, a few days after his felonious scheme was concluded."

Though it was not a surprise, I was still amazed that Duncan had convinced Junior to go along with this *schmegegge* story. It was a certainty that Junior would serve a life sentence in maximum prison with a guilty plea corroborated with a detailed confession, likely worded by Duncan and his legal team. Coercing London to corroborate Junior's confession with perjured testimony was overkill and added unnecessary risk to everyone involved. However, it was to be expected. Duncan never worried about risk and consequence. Even while committing a felony, Duncan put on a show to remember.

2.

"No one could have seen it coming," Duncan lied as solemnly as possible.

"Mr. Thomas, every individual involved in the murder, and subsequent attempted cover-up, was close to you. Additionally, Joel Lewinsky, who admitted to having stolen millions of dollars from your business partners and the taxpayers, has literally signed off with nearly every deal you ever participated in, including the contract for the building where we are currently conducting this very interview," Chase responded.

"I barely knew him. Before this whole thing, I forgot what he even looked like." Duncan shrugged.

"There are literally hundreds of photos of the two of you together dating back at least fifteen years ago," Chase said with an exasperated smile.

"Listen, Chase, don't be a cutie-pie. I told you, I barely knew the guy."

"What about your eldest son, Duncan Thomas Jr.? Surely, there had to be some indication that he was stealing from you as well. And he was dating your mistress when you had your affair with her while she was pregnant with your biological grandson."

"My son is a good person, okay? He means well, but he is guilty. He did everything, and he admitted it already. He said I didn't know about it, and what is important to remember is that I didn't know anything about it. And another thing I want to tell you, he is really guilty, and I am not, okay?"

Chase shook his head in equal parts frustration and confusion, unable to respond to the masterful gibberish answer he'd just received.

"Mr. Thomas, what about Sarah Verand?"

"Terrific reporter, very talented individual."

"She was murdered—"

"A tragedy." Duncan nodded obliviously.

"She was murdered writing a story about you."

"If you say so. I know nothing about it."

"There is a tape of your personal lawyer, Max Cedar, verbally abusing and threatening her if she continued to write the story about your affair with London and presumably about your son's affair also."

"Max Cedar was one of many lawyers who represented me. He is a liar and a fraud. To be honest, I barely knew the guy."

"You barely knew your personal attorney?"

"To be honest, he did very little work for me for a few years. He is a nobody trying to pretend he is a big-time lawyer. The man is a loser."

I threw down my cell phone in a rage. Curse words flew out of my mouth toward Duncan, who now appeared with a fresh crack splitting his fat face on my phone's damaged screen. Zevi ran to the other room after opportunistically taking the rest of the bagel to eat elsewhere. Before I knew it, I fell to the floor, unable to get myself off it on my own. That con man kept fucking me at every turn. I'd outfoxed that two-bit hustler at his own game, yet he still got to have the last laugh.

3

It was so hot in my father's apartment I was already shvitzing before I even took my coat off.

"Susan, the place looks great! The Seder table is just beautiful!" Vivian exclaimed as she quickly hugged Susan and handed her a bottle of kosher white wine from the vineyards of Jerusalem. None of my family kept kosher, but when celebrating Passover in New York, it was expected everyone pretended to be.

"Susan, I'm dying over here. It's so hot I feel like I literally walked the desert for forty years," I told her as I put my coat away.

"Oh, I know; it's hotter in here than noon on the Fourth of July. You know how your father is, always complaining about how cold it is. Personally, I don't mind. It feels like home for me." Susan smiled. "I'll put it down for you. I thought you'd be used to it living in sunny California for so long," Susan said.

"I lived on the other side of California. Is he still in his room?" I asked.

"Oh, go right on in. I'll be in the living room giving the kids their presents." Susan motioned me away.

"Presents are for Hanukkah. There are no presents given at Passover—"

"Go away! The kids want presents, and we want to drink the wine already!" Vivian interrupted me, winking at Susan while shoving me toward the other room.

"Who's there?" my father asked after I knocked several times.

"It's Max," I shouted through the door.

"Max?" my father yelled back.

"It's Max! Your son!"

"You think I don't know who my son is?"

"Can I just come in?"

"Come in already! What's with all the yelling?"

Isaac sat at the edge of his bed reading a Haggadah, the religious text read at the Passover dinner. For his age, he looked physically well. My father had inherited the fighting spirit of his father, who received it from his father. I couldn't help but believe it was that same spirit that had gotten me through this mess with Duncan. Despite the horrible decisions I had made in my life, when I relied on my fight-or-flight instinct, I was able to do what was needed to survive.

"You remember this one?" Isaac asked, holding up the Haggadah book.

"It's the one we read when I was a kid," I replied. The cover was dusty and faded, but the pages were crisp, and the Hebrew print was still legible.

"Can you still read it?" Isaac asked, raising his eyebrows.

"It has been a while, but I think I could manage."

"Manage is good. Knowing is better," he commented. I continued to look through the book before my father said, "I saw your dog-shit boss on the computer."

"I had no idea you even knew how to do that," I said.

"Susan put it on. You know, he really is dog shit."

"I remember you saying that ten seconds ago."

"Do you know how much better I feel now that you are not working for that horrible creature?"

"I have some idea. I also feel better."

"Of course you do! I said you would, didn't I?"

"You were right. I should have listened to you."

"Can you believe my son telling me he should have listened to his father?" My father laughed. I helped my father up, and as he exited the room, he turned around, put his hand on my shoulder, and said, "Today we celebrate the Hebrews escaping slavery from the evil pharaoh and you escaping slavery from the evil Duncan. I don't even want to tell you who I think is worse."

4.

The Haggadah describes how the Hebrew slaves endured the horrifying consequences of the Ten Plagues, fled for their lives from the mighty Egyptian army, and then suffered a devastating forty-year detour in the Sinai Desert. However, not a single individual who had crossed the Red Sea entered the Promised Land. Not even Moses. If I had been the Hebrews' lawyer back then, I would have sued the Almighty for breaking the verbal contract promising entrance into Israel. Based on my experience with Duncan, though, I also would have been one of the first to worship the golden calf.

"You already going?" my father asked.

"We finished the whole thing already, Pop," I replied.

"Really, Mr. Rabbi? Then why did we not open the door for the prophet Eliyahu?" he asked, pointing his finger at the door.

Though it was a blatant cover-up attempt for his lapse of memory, he was factually correct. Every Passover, it was tradition to open the door symbolically for the prophet Elijah's spirit to enter. There was even a full cup of wine at his (empty) seat.

"We must have forgotten. We will do it next year."

"Passover Seder cannot be over until we leave the door open for Eliyahu!" my father demanded with a sudden surge of energy that could only come from a determination not to be wrong.

"Okay, we will open the door for the prophet, even though every year he never shows up," I said, shaking my head.

"So you are a comedian and a rabbi now?"

I walked over to the door and, looking in the direction of my father, opened the door and loudly pronounced, "I am opening the door now for Elijah, OK? Here, it is open now."

"Max Cedar," a male adult voice responded. Confused, I turned around slowly, half believing it was actually a spirit.

"Yes," I replied, seeing it was a white man in a work suit.

"I am Special Agent McCamel of the FBI. You need to come with us," the man replied, displaying his badge.

"What the hell for?" I was in the clear. No way the feds, or anyone, had anything connecting me to Junior or London or even Duncan.

"Witness intimidation and obstruction of justice," the man said as he motioned for me to turn around, an order with which I compulsively complied.

"What is this all about? Where do these charges stem from?" I asked as the cuffs were put on me.

"The Richard Sand case. He has confessed and told us what you made him do," the agent replied.

"The fucking wobbler case? I can't believe this shit!"

"Max, what is going on?" Vivian asked, rushing to the door.

"I'll explain later," I replied. "Get a lawyer to meet me at whatever station they are taking me to. And a doctor. I think I am having a stroke."

"So who was at the door?" I heard my father ask. "Eliyahu?"

Epilogue

Richard had made a deal with the feds. By turning me in for witness intimidation, they dismissed the initial assault charge against him. He got community service for his part of the alleged obstruction of justice. I realized, much too late, that this had been Duncan's plan B from the beginning. I should have known better than to think I was going to cross Duncan without any punishment from him. Duncan always sought retribution. I thought I'd crossed him up to the point where he couldn't strike back. I was very wrong.

Back in San Francisco, I had been found guilty by a jury of my peers and was awaiting sentencing from the judge. As unfair as this whole charade was, I was lucky to have such an honorable judge presiding over the case. The irony of being sentenced to prison for a crime I did not commit while evading any judicial punishment for all the guilty acts I had committed on behalf of Duncan in the past was too much to bear. My only hope now was that the judge would show some mercy on my sentencing.

Judge Emmett Coolings was a short and bald African American. He did not tolerate nonsense and had a clear sense of justice. He stared directly at me for his closing remarks.

"I've listened to all this, and it's very painful. You made a lot of mistakes, Mr. Cedar. The saddest part of this whole thing is that some very innocent people are hurting too—your family. I don't know where you go from here. For whatever reason, it sounds like you got caught up in it. Hopefully, going to prison will lead to a better Max Cedar. Hopefully, you will show society you can change and that you can be better. With that, the court sentences the accused to eighteen months in a federal prison. The court is adjourned."

I was sent straight to prison from the courthouse after I was sentenced. By the time I arrived at the upstate penitentiary, I was full of emotions. I was angry with Duncan and Richard for framing me for a crime I had no part of and being sent to jail because of it. However, I considered that eighteen months could be seen as a fair punishment for all the illegal and immoral acts I had done in the past. Most of all, I was sad that I'd let my family down. They'd said they would stand by me through this whole mess, and for that, I could not be more grateful.

Before I even got my cell assigned, a guard yelled my name and said I had a call. When I picked up the receiver, I heard Duncan's voice booming in my ear.

"You almost did it, Max. But I had to put you down for a bit. It is just the way it had to be. I am very impressed with how you handled yourself. When you get out, come back to work for me. Clean slate. I'm thinking of entering politics. These corrupt clowns in Washington have no idea what they're doing. Time to clean the swamp, Max, and I want you beside me. You're still my fixer."

I hung up the phone in a daze. The thought of Duncan as the most powerful person in the world was too horrifying to comprehend.